"Katie, ␣

The truth? ␣␣␣ ␣␣␣␣␣␣␣␣␣␣␣␣
the full reas␣␣␣␣␣␣␣␣␣␣␣␣ to Blossom Grove? But how
could he know about her past? Or know everything
that had happened to her?

Heart pounding, she attempted to sound calm. "I'm
not sure what you mean, Nathan."

"I'm talking about the market closing early most days."

"Oh, *jah*, that." Exhaling softly, her pulse began to slow
itself.

"Can we set aside some time to talk about that?"

"Of course. The sooner the better. It was on my list to
go over with you, trust me."

Trust me? Could she really say that to anyone?

As they walked back into the office to talk with Abram,
she couldn't stop from worrying. Nor could she stop
hearing those words reverberating in her mind. She
was so weary from keeping secrets of her past. But
didn't she have to in order to secure her future?

Cathy Liggett is an Ohio girl who never dreamed her writing journey would take her across the world and to Amish country, too. But she's learned God's plans for our lives are greater and more creative than the ones we often imagine for ourselves. That includes meeting her husband at a high school reunion and marrying three months later—nearly forty years ago. Together, they enjoy visiting kids and grandkids and spoiling their pup, Chaz.

Books by Cathy Liggett

Love Inspired

Her Secret Amish Match
Trusting Her Amish Heart
Their Unlikely Amish Courtship
Secrets of Her Amish Heart

Visit the Author Profile page at LoveInspired.com.

SECRETS OF HER AMISH HEART

CATHY LIGGETT

LOVE INSPIRED
INSPIRATIONAL ROMANCE

LOVE INSPIRED®
INSPIRATIONAL ROMANCE

ISBN-13: 978-1-335-62108-5

Secrets of Her Amish Heart

Recycling programs for this product may not exist in your area.

Love Inspired
22 Adelaide St. West, 41st Floor
Toronto, Ontario M5H 4E3, Canada
www.LoveInspired.com

Printed in Lithuania

MIX
Paper | Supporting responsible forestry
FSC® C021394

But they that wait upon the Lord shall renew their
strength; they shall mount up with wings as eagles;
they shall run, and not be weary;
and they shall walk, and not faint.
—*Isaiah* 40:31

To my loving and caring sister Patty.

It may sound so simple, but know the feelings
run deep when I say, thank you for
always being there for me.

Chapter One

April showers bring May flowers.

As Katie Troyer walked down the main street of Blossom Grove toward Miller's Market to work, the saying echoed in her mind. The adage used to sound like such a hopeful statement throughout much of her life. But right this minute? That expression was simply frustrating. And while she knew she didn't deserve special treatment from *Gott*, even so, she begged Him to at least hold off on the rain for a few more minutes. Just until she got to where she was going.

Immediately, however, her request was followed up with yet another rumbling overhead. Was *Gott* saying her plans were not His plans? It sure seemed that way. That was even more apparent when the early morning sky suddenly turned as gray as a stormy nightfall. Moments later, trickles of rain began to dot the sidewalk. Before she knew it, she was skipping around even larger droplets, and plenty of them.

Oh, if only she'd asked to borrow an umbrella from Mary Louise! That would've been extremely helpful since she hadn't brought much more than the clothes on her back when she and her sister Annie moved—or rather escaped—to this quaint little town in Holmes County, Ohio. For sure and certain, the sweet owner of the Happy Endings Inn where she and Annie had been staying for the past several weeks would've been glad to lend her one. Even so, why would she have bothered to ask Mary Louise? There hadn't been even a hint of rain when she first left the inn. Of course, she should know better than anyone how quickly life, love, the weather—mostly everything—can change on a person in a flash. Shouldn't she?

Feeling beads of rain dampen the black sweater her *mamm* had knitted for her so many years ago, her shoulders began to sag. If her adoptive parents were still alive, what would they think of the mess she'd gotten herself and her sister into? The question gnawed at her like it always did, causing her soul to ache. Yet, she knew that constantly reliving all that had happened wasn't healthy or helpful. She needed to work hard and do something about the here and now. She needed to do everything by the book, and not by her heart ever again. And she would. Her fourteen-year-old sister deserved as much.

Fortunately, almost as soon as she and Annie had arrived in Blossom Grove, Mary Louise seemed to sense they needed help. Right away, she'd introduced Katie to Sylvia and after a brief interview, the job at Sylvia's brother's market was hers. Since she agreed to get there early to make sure everything was in place each day, Sylvia had trusted her to do just that and turned over the store keys to her. But the thought struck her that Sylvia had also trusted her to do other things too, hadn't she?

Placing her cloth handbag over her *kapp*-covered head, she purposefully quickened her steps. Then she broke into an all-out jog, trying to ignore the rainwater splashing at the hem of her navy cotton dress. As soon as she reached the outside of the market's front door, she removed the moist handbag from atop her head and straightened her soggy *kapp*.

She swiped at the drenched fallen hairs on her forehead before fumbling in her wet bag for the market's keychain. Sifting through the keys, she easily found the one she was looking for. Leaning forward, she was about to insert it into the lock, when suddenly she was aware of a protective canopy covering her head, shutting out the rain. She smiled and relief came over her like a ray of sunshine. Without a doubt, there was only person who'd be arriving around the same time who'd be kind enough to share an umbrella.

"Oh, Sylvia, *danke*," she said, turning to look behind her. As she did, she gasped. Instead of seeing the woman who had hired her, she looked right up into the compelling blue eyes of a man she'd never seen before.

"You're—you're not Sylvia," she stuttered, trying not to panic. "Not the owner's sister."

"Hardly." The man's lips crooked into a smile causing dimples to charmingly dot his cheeks. There might've been a time in her life that she would've been impressed by such good looks. But that time had passed. And she'd promised herself it would never come again. Trying to put a distance between the two of them, she stepped back. But he only moved closer, hovering the umbrella over her head.

Nervously, she cleared her throat. "Sir, we don't officially open for another half hour."

During her training session with the married sixty-or-so-year-old Sylvia, Katie had jotted down everything she was saying in a little notebook, which fit right into her apron pocket. In fact, Sylvia had complimented her desire to be accurate and precise. But along with her entries regarding everything Sylvia had mentioned about the cash register, stocking shelves, discarding dated items, keeping an accounting, along with a dozen other notes, there was another item. One that Katie had underlined twice. And that, as Sylvia had stated, was the main goal of the market—to please customers. To that end, even with her insides shaking, Katie looked at the man standing opposite her and faked a courteous smile. "You're more than welcome to come back when we're open to customers," she told him. "I'll be happy to help you then."

Still, the man didn't move. He only dipped his head, wavy light brown hair poking out from his dry straw hat. "I'm familiar with the store hours."

Then why was he still standing there? "So, you know we're still closed to customers." She repeated herself, her tone turning a bit less pleasant.

"I do."

Even saying so, he stood firmly. Her heart quickened, and she wondered how to get away from him. She wasn't about to unlock the door with him standing there. No way did she want to be in the store with him by herself at this point. Of course, standing nearly toe to toe under the umbrella wasn't so comfortable either.

But then again, would a man who was potentially dangerous carry a bright neon yellow umbrella? Also, would he be wearing a splint on his right wrist? Or was it all a disguise? *Gott* knew she'd been fooled by a man's appearance before.

Oh, Sylvia, where are you?

Slanting her head to look around him, she glanced down the puddled sidewalk, hoping to see the woman. Not surprisingly, with the rain pouring harder than ever, the walkway was nearly void of people.

"Sylvia isn't coming." The man seemed to read her mind.

"She's not?"

"*Nee.* And I'm sorry if I frightened you." His eyes turned sympathetic. "I was just trying to be helpful when I saw you didn't have an umbrella. I'm Nathan, by the way. Nathan Bowman. Sylvia is my *aenti* and her *bruder* Jacob, the market's owner is—"

"Your *onkel*?" she blurted.

"*Jah*. My great *onkel*." He paused, gazing at her. "And you're Katie, right? Sylvia said you're new in town and from Tuscarawas County. She also said that you're a great worker."

Inwardly, she smiled at that.

"I used to work here as a teenager, and I know all about the market," he continued. "Since I'm back in town for a short stay, she asked if I'd help you out."

She knew Sylvia had had a lot on her plate lately. Yet, instantly she missed her employer and coworker. Outwardly, she worked hard to conceal a frown.

Apparently, he noticed. "Well, um, why don't we get out of this rain?" he suggested. "You probably want to get dried off. And then we can get to work."

Before she knew what was happening, he quickly and somewhat rudely in her estimation, shoved the umbrella handle into her hand before she could refuse it. With his good hand free, he grasped the keychain from her. She knew it wasn't kind of her, but she did feel somewhat smug watching this person who "knew all about the store" grapple with the keys. After a minute or so, she let him in on her secret.

"I color-coded the keys," she informed him.

"You did what?" It was his turn to look perplexed.

"I purchased those plastic colored covers for the keys at the hardware store. So, you'll find the key with the orange cover is for the front door. *O* for orange and *o* for the door that gets opened to the public. Get it? And then, the key with the blue cover is for the back door of the market.

B and *b*. There's purple, red, green, and yellow too," she added. "But no need to know about those keys and colors right this minute. If you're interested later, I have it all written down right here in my notebook." She patted her apron pocket where she always kept it handy.

Sylvia had been impressed by her color-coded key system. But obviously, Nathan didn't appreciate her thoroughness or think she was clever at all. At least he didn't act like he did. Rather, he simply stared at her and blinked as if she was from another universe altogether. Heat flooded her cheeks.

"Like you said, we should get inside." She nodded toward the door.

After unlocking the door, he at least politely held it open for her to go first. Closing the umbrella, she handed it back to him and slipped inside. The awkwardness between them continued when they both went to flip on the store lights simultaneously. Her hand clumsily knocked into his splint-covered wrist.

"I'm so sorry. I really am," she apologized, feeling awful. "Did that hurt?"

She noticed him gulp as he hugged the wrist to his chest. Even so, instead of carrying on like a baby, he answered like a man. "Naw. It'll be okay. I know you didn't mean to do it." He may or may not have realized it, but even as he said the words, his left brow rose, questioningly.

"I truly didn't," she answered. "Honest." To prove it, she offered her assistance. "Here, let me get the umbrella from you. And your hat too."

After a slight pause, he deposited both into her outstretched hands, giving her a thankful nod. She was grateful as well. It was nice to have an opportunity to part ways from this stranger, even if only momentarily. As was her custom each morning, she headed to the back of the store and hung his items on a wall rack and left her damp sweater there to dry.

That small task complete, she was all ready to get settled in by the cash register. But Nathan had beat her to it. Looking puzzled, he stood at the front counter, staring at the machine, scratching the top of his thick head of hair.

"This is new," he stated. "Nothing like when I used to work here."

"It was new to me too. Sylvia told me they switched to a computerized system over a year ago. But it's really easy to use. You just—"

She tapped the screen and a box came up. "This is where I put in my employee ID and password. Then it's all set to go."

"Password and ID? Hmm…" He frowned. "I mostly do carpentry work. I've never been in a position to have to use anything computerized."

"Me neither until now." Curious, she looked up at him. "Do you work nearby?"

"In Middlefield."

"That's far from here, isn't it?"

"About a hundred miles away."

"Oh." She wondered how he'd managed to get a job that far away and even how he'd injured his wrist. But it wasn't any of her business just like where she'd come from and why she was in Blossom Grove wasn't any concern of his.

"For now, may I use your ID and password? I figure I'll mainly be the one at the cash register. I can do light activities with this." He waved his splinted wrist in the air. "But if you could help bag when possible, when you're not helping customers, that would be *gut*. And I'll try to do the same. What I can't do is run the meat and cheese slicers. Can you?"

She nodded. "I'll do whatever it takes to make the place run smoothly," she replied, meaning every word. For the store's sake and her own.

"So, um…" She hesitated. "When is Sylvia coming back? I mean, she is coming back, ain't so?" she asked and hoped.

Tilting his head, he let go of a long sigh. "I guess you know my great *onkel*'s history, don't you? How he recently lost his wife of thirty-five years? Sold his home and moved into Sylvia and her husband Clyde's house? And then had to have heart surgery?"

"*Jah*, I do. I've been including him in my prayers," she said, truthfully. "And I believe that's why Sylvia hired me."

"Well, as you can imagine with all that, plus Clyde's sometimes debilitating sciatica, I think Sylvia is just plain tired. Worn out. So, she made a decision. She's not coming back to work."

While Katie's heart did go out to the dear woman, hearing that, it also sank.

"While I'm in town, she's asked me to hire a replacement for her. Another employee," Nathan continued. "And…" He looked her directly in the eye. "In the meantime, I'll also be overseeing you."

Overseeing her? Did that really come out of the mouth of the man who didn't know which key opened the market's door? Who had no clue how to operate the cash register? And who didn't even have two good hands to slice meats and cheeses? Would he honestly even be able to manage bagging groceries?

"Why, that sounds…" *Verrickt.* Crazy. And somewhat of a rude way to put it.

She wanted to say all those things. But she swallowed hard and didn't dare. She couldn't. Not when she'd promised Annie that one day soon, they'd go from nearly penniless to having a nice place of their own again. No matter how much hard work it took, she owed that to her sister. Plus, she owed something to Mary Louise and Sylvia for their help too. "That sounds…" she repeated "…*wunderbaar*."

She tried to exclaim the word in an upbeat, positive way. Yet, even to her own ears, her voice fell flat. Right away, she plastered a phony smile on her face. Hopefully, her new boss wouldn't detect her lack of sincerity and glee. But then why would he? He certainly hadn't noticed anything else about her. Like how she'd been overseeing *him* ever since they'd walked in the door.

Nathan knew that earlier he might've seemed somewhat idiotic standing out in the rain, holding an umbrella over Katie's head and barely uttering a word. But that was only because he'd been shocked when she had turned around to face him. Yes, his *aenti* had said what a dedicated worker Katie Troyer was. But she never once hinted that the ivory-skinned blonde girl was so pretty. Obviously, he wasn't expecting her attractive upturned blue eyes to be looking into his. And so close! He hadn't been able to stop staring.

This time, however, standing across from her and seeing the expression on her face, he wasn't an idiot. Not at all. She may have said the word *wunderbaar* out loud, but he knew she didn't mean it. There was no liveliness in her voice. No light in her smile. Hard as she was trying, she couldn't hide her disappointment. Seeing that, he cringed.

"Katie, I, uh, I might've said that all wrong." He offered an olive branch, but she didn't appear ready to take it. She'd already moved on, busily straightening containers of blueberries in the refrigerated bin opposite the entrance.

"You said what you needed to." She gave him a quick glance over her shoulder.

"*Jah*, but I should've been—" *More delicate?* Was that a good thing to say? Or would that be suggesting he didn't perceive her to be a strong woman?

Not having a clue how to complete the sentence, he clamped his mouth shut. Plain and simple, he wasn't used to working with women. In Middlefield at Shetler's Home-builders, the men worked together as a team. And during voluntary search and rescue missions, the same was true. The last time he worked with a woman was forever ago at the market with *Onkel* Jacob's wife, Lovina. And she was his *aenti*. So, that didn't really count, did it?

And the last time he'd been in a relationship with a woman…

Regrettably, his mind drifted to Sarah Lapp, now Sarah Fisher. The girl who'd been one of the reasons he'd packed a bag and left Blossom Grove for good two years earlier. But how could he blame her for what she'd done? Just like her, he hadn't been honest. Even so, walking down the main street of town the past couple of days, a feeling of dread tightened his stomach at the thought of running into her again. He was glad when Katie turned to him, interrupting his stewing.

"I have a question for you." She crossed her arms over her waist.

"Feel free to ask." That sounded kind and friendly, didn't it?

"When you do interviews, may I sit in on them? After all, I'll be the one working with that person. And you'll be leaving."

Did he detect a slight smile crossing her lips when she spoke of his imminent departure? He was pretty sure he did. Even so, he pushed that possibility aside and answered nicely. "*Jah*, of course. That makes perfect sense."

"*Danke,*" she replied.

"Oh, and *Aenti* Sylvia did say she's already spoken to one person who will be coming in for an interview tomorrow," he informed her. "Also, I'm going to put a sign in the window saying that we're hiring."

"*Gut. Verra gut.*"

For a change, she looked pleased with him, which pleased him too. But the somewhat amiable atmosphere in the store didn't last long. The bell over the front door jangled, and Mrs. Mildred Hochstetler made her way into the market.

How did he get so unfortunate to have her as his first customer? He groaned. Then feigned great pleasure in seeing the often cranky, brusque older woman.

"Mrs. Hochstetler, it's so nice to see you. *Gut* morning to you."

"*Gut?* It's still drizzling out there." She swiped droplets off her cape. Then dipping her head, she peered over her glasses, looking him up and down. "I see you're back."

"For a short while, *jah*."

"Humph." She quirked a brow. "I suppose that's *gut*."

He wasn't sure if she meant it was good that he was back, or good that he was leaving again. Although, given his history with Mrs. Hochstetler, he suspected it was the latter. The woman had never seemed to forgive him when, at age eleven, he and his friend had a somewhat mischievous lack of judgment where her juicy red tomatoes were concerned. And fifteen years later, Mrs. Hochstetler still didn't look pleased to lay eyes on him. Yet, she was the customer, and he was at her service. He tried again.

"So, what may I help you with this morning?" he asked courteously.

"You? Nothing." She shook her head. "Katie knows exactly what I'm here for."

Apparently, after just a few weeks of working there, his coworker had readily recognized Mrs. Hochstetler's distinctive voice. She scurried up the aisle and came to the woman's side. "Mrs. Hochstetler, you're our first customer of the day and what a delight. Are you here for your usual meat and cheese order this morning?"

"I am, dear girl."

"Oh, *gut*. Come on over to the deli counter, and I'll get that prepared for you. And, in the meantime, you can tell me all about your visit with your grandchildren this past weekend."

Watching Katie in action, he had to admit he was impressed. Mrs. Hochstetler lit up like he'd never seen before. Thankfully, he and his coworker hadn't been involved in a customer-service contest. If they had, Katie would've surely won this time around, hands down.

Oh, well. Four more weeks…and his wrist would be healed. That would be his victory.

Come summer, I'll be back in Middlefield for good.

He sighed and glanced out the window into the wet haze. To be sure, there wasn't anything for him in Blossom Grove. Nothing except reminders of things gone wrong. For him and because of him.

It was doubtful anyone had missed him since he'd been gone, but townsfolk would surely miss Miller's Market if it no longer existed. Decade upon decade, his aunt and uncle's market had been praised. And the store truly deserved its fine reputation for quality, friendliness, and for the part it played in helping the community. It had been disheartening to visibly see how the store's appearance wasn't up to par, inside and out. And hearing from Sylvia how the business was waning, moved him too. He might only have a month, but he promised himself to do everything he could to make the store what it used to be. That was going to be a big job, physically and—

Mentally. He looked down at the state-of-the-art cash register. Just seeing it brought on a wave of distress.

With his good hand, he rubbed at the tense knot in his right shoulder. It'd been irritated ever since he'd fallen down a ravine and sprained his wrist. Of course, sleeping on his *aenti* Sylvia's love seat the last two nights hadn't helped his shoulder either. But he hadn't had a choice. Unable to predict his unexpected homecoming, his parents had rented out their house while traveling around the country to see their grandbabies.

Thankfully, starting tonight, he had another alternative for a place to stay. From the time he'd woken up stiff and sore that morning, he'd been looking forward to the end of the workday. It was going to be *wunderbaar*, to use Katie's word, to settle in at a place that had always been so special to him. A sanctuary where he could relax and heal on his hours off work. And best of all—he glanced at Katie and Mrs. Hochstetler tittering together over at the deli counter—not be bothered by a soul.

But until then…

Taking a deep breath, he began to scan all the options on the cash register screen in front of him.

Things in the world were always changing, weren't they? But was it ever for the better?

Chapter Two

"One day down…"

Katie had been thinking the exact same thing when Nathan muttered the comment as they stood outside the front door of the market ten hours later. As he slipped the orange covered key in the slot to lock up for the day, she didn't respond verbally. But a sound did escape from her. A sigh of relief that the day was done.

How many more days would she have to be working with him? He'd mentioned to her that he'd be in town for a month. Was that a month with thirty days, or thirty-one?

"Your idea about color-coding the keys is a *gut* one," he said, dangling the keychain of rainbow hues in the air.

Instantly, her mouth dropped open. His compliment did more than take her by surprise. It shocked her. She hadn't heard much from him all day, except when he was correcting her about something.

But maybe, at day's end, outside the market, this was the start of a new way of communicating between them. Was that possible? If so, she wasn't about to put a damper on it.

"I appreciate you saying so, Nathan," she replied. "And I think you had some good ideas yourself today."

His dark blue eyes brightened, looking delighted to hear that. "*Jah?* Like what?"

"Oh, you know." She hesitated, scratching her head, not at all sure what to say. "You, uh, you schooled me on cleaning the meat slicer." As if she hadn't already known. "And even how you helped me clean up the jars of relish that Iva Yoder dropped."

Seeing his mouth gape this time, she was sure he'd been expecting something more from her. Clueless as to what else to say, her eyes drifted from his. Fortunately, they landed on the store window.

"And the now-hiring sign." She pointed. "It's *gut* you got that up," she added.

However, if he'd only asked her, she would've done a much better job with the lettering. Undoubtedly, it would've been a task that Sylvia would've turned over to her. But then Sylvia had trusted her to do a fine job in every way. Even from the very beginning, she'd never felt like the woman was looking over her shoulder every hour of the day, scrutinizing her every move.

Needless to say, that wasn't so with Nathan. Not only that, but even though there was an age gap with Sylvia, the two of them could talk about recipes and girl stuff when they weren't overwhelmed with customers. Whereas, working with a man, she wasn't sure what to say. And she felt like she had to pretend to stay busy even when they weren't.

But…only twenty-nine more days to go. Or was it going to be thirty?

"I don't know how many people will apply for the job," Nathan said frankly. "But if you still want to sit in on the interview tomorrow, I told Abram Lytle to be here a half hour before we open."

"Not a problem. I'm always at the market then anyway. That's why Sylvia had given me a set of keys." She thought that might prompt him to return the keychain to her. Instead, he grasped it more tightly in his hand. Perhaps to demonstrate he was in control? Or was her past with a man causing her to overreact in the present?

"All right, I'll see you then." Nathan nodded a goodbye.

With that, Katie thought they'd part ways. Rather, they began walking down the sidewalk in the same direction. After passing the hardware store, the florist, the bakery and the antique shop in an uncomfortable silence, she felt the need to say something. Anything.

"At least the sun is out now," she said.

"Yeah. No need for an umbrella."

Her face flushed, recalling their close encounter that morning. She assumed he must've remembered the same incident when his footing faltered. And he cleared his throat.

"I forgot I wanted to make a stop back there." He pointed over his shoulder. "See you later."

"*Jah.* See you."

Whew! That's all she could think when he finally turned from her. The awkwardness between them had made the day exhausting. Plodding one tired foot in front of the other, her mood did brighten some when she cast her eyes on the Happy Endings Inn a block ahead. It was easy to see that the bothersome April showers had lent an early start on spring blooms. Golden daffodils lined the walkway. Grape-colored hyacinths surrounded and complemented the inn's sign with its carved name and bow, painted sky blue and white to match the house. No doubt the tulips currently breaking ground would give the other flowers something to compete with come May. And that was just the front of the brown-roofed inn. In the rear of the two-story country home, Mary Louise had planted several colorfully painted birdhouses on every side of her garden area. Just like the inn provided a happy haven for guests and townsfolk, those stood ready to provide the same for feathered friends. Over-all, the outside of the inn couldn't have been any lovelier or more welcoming.

Whereas on the inside of the inn...

As she reached her destination and began to climb the inn's wooden stairs, a familiar anxiousness came with each step. Her unease had nothing to do with Mary Louise. The widowed woman couldn't have been more steadfast and delightful. From the first time she'd seen Mary Louise Eicher, she'd instantly been drawn in by the inn owner's cheerful gait. The way the woman walked so buoyantly it was as if she couldn't wait to see what *Gott* had in store for her next. And who she might help next. No way could Katie have ever imagined a more wonderful person to keep Annie company and busy working each day. For that, she was overwhelmingly thankful to Mary Louise and *Gott.*

Yet, her sister on the other hand, well... In Annie's defense, she had been through a lot in her short life. Beyond that, she was a teenager. Like most teens, her mood could shift from sweet to prickly or silly to sage-like in the snap of a finger. Because of that, Katie took a deep breath as she entered the inn. Who knew what to expect?

A rustling sound from the kitchen led her in that direction. There she saw Annie stirring a bowl of icing beside a platter of cupcakes on the wooden island. When her sister was a young *kind,* Katie used to automatically greet her with a kiss on top of her *kapp*-covered head. In return, Annie would give her a sweet caress around her waist. Or gift her with a happy smile. And although Katie would've still attempted the same kind of hello by standing on her tiptoes since Annie was close to her height now, she knew better than to try. These days her affection didn't get at all the same reaction it used to years ago. Instead, Annie often backed away. But at least Katie could still utter the nickname she'd given her sister. One that *used to* make Annie laugh. Her sister couldn't stop her from doing that.

"Hey, Annie Bananie. I missed you. How's the day been?"

Her hazel-eyed sister gave her a pensive look, and Katie stiffened. How she missed the days of youthful joy always shining in her sister's eyes!

"The day has been, I don't know. It's just been, I guess." Annie shrugged, setting down the bowl.

"What all did you do?"

Annie tucked her hands into her apron pockets. "Nothing much different. Since it rained most of the day, Mary Louise and I couldn't get to any gardening. It's been a day of cleaning, cooking, baking and…well…reflection."

Reflection? Katie's chest tightened. When had her sister learned such a word?

"You mean reflecting on which dessert to make?" Katie tried to make light of the subject.

Annie wasn't having it. "There you go again, Katie." She crossed her arms over her chest. "You may be ten years older than me, and, *jah*, you've told me a hundred times how you played house with me from the time I was two and pretended to be my mom. And you've been a *mamm* to me ever since *Mamm* and *Daed* went to be with the Lord. And it ain't like I'm not thankful. But sometimes I wish you'd just be a friend. Because here in this place you moved us to, I don't have any. I wish you'd listen to me and take me seriously."

Hearing the emotion in Annie's voice, Katie tried to swallow back her own. "I'm sorry, Annie. It just…" *It breaks my heart when I hear yours doing the same.* She stepped forward to brush a wisp of hair from Annie's forehead. This time, praise *Gott*, Annie didn't step away. "I do take you seriously, Annie. Please tell me. What were you reflecting on?"

"It doesn't matter." Annie shook her head. "It's nothing that can be fixed."

"Maybe not. But can you share with me? Please?" *Let me in.*

"Oll recht, oll recht." Annie flung her arms in the air. "I realized today that I'm older now. And it's what I always wanted to be. Or I thought I did. But now I don't want to be this age. With no school and no friends to see every day, I feel kind of—"

"Lost?" Katie interjected. "And like growing up isn't all it's cracked up to be?"

"Well, *jah*." Annie looked surprised. "And, I don't know if I want to be cleaning and cooking my whole life 'cause it feels like that's all I'm doing now."

"And you don't only have to do those things," Katie promptly replied. No way did she want her sister to settle for less than everything she could ever be. "Annie, you're a smart girl and you have a warm caring heart. When you want to, that is." She teased with a wink. "But seriously, take each day and grow from it. Maybe one day you'll want to run an inn like this. Or, you love *kinner*. Maybe you'll be a teacher or a nanny. You're great at baking too. Who knows? You could have your own bakery someday. In fact, maybe we can even sell some of your goods at the market."

"Really, Katie?" Finally, a spark lit in her sister's eyes.

"Well, possibly." Sylvia wouldn't have minded that. But who knew about Nathan? She almost wished she hadn't mentioned the possibility. "And, Annie, I should've told you that since you've been so helpful to Mary Louise around here, she's not only giving you a bit of money to save. She's also giving us a reduced rate at the inn."

"Oh." Annie's shoulders straightened. "I guess I'm doing more than I thought."

"*Jah*, you are. Plus, you made my favorite cupcakes. Red velvet. Did you use *Mamm*'s recipe?"

Her sister nodded. "I wasn't only missing friends today. I was really missing *Mamm* and *Daed* too. I baked them so I could feel close to her. Well, to them." She paused, her eyes turning misty. "Remember how *Daed* used to come into the kitchen and stick his fingers into the batter? And *Mamm* would scold him, then give him a heaping spoon-ful?" She chuckled with a sniffle.

"Oh, Annie. *Jah*, I do remember." Katie pulled her sister into her arms. "*Danke* for baking the cupcakes, *schweschder*. I mean it. I always miss *Mamm* and *Daed*, and you baking those helps me too." She stroked Annie's *kapp*-covered head. "I hope you know I'll always be here for you," she whispered.

"I do." Annie hugged her back. "And I hope you know the cupcakes aren't only here for you."

"Ha!" Katie laughed as they broke apart. "I promise I won't forget that." She crossed her heart and swiped at her cheeks. Then grew concerned that Annie might ask if she missed the other person who'd recently passed from their lives—Jonathan Lantz.

She quickly changed the subject. "Where's Mary Louise, by the way? I smell something good coming from the oven."

"That's the casserole we made for dinner tonight. But she got sauce all over her dress and went upstairs to get cleaned up."

"Is there anything I can help you with?"

"I just finished making buttercream frosting. If you want, you can help me ice the cupcakes."

"I'd love to. I just need to wash my hands first."

Feeling heartened that they'd been able to share a closeness again, she went over to the sink and turned on the water. She didn't know what made her look out the window. But she did. And froze. Was she imagining things? She leaned over the sink to get a closer look.

"Oh, I can't believe it," she murmured.

"Believe what?" Annie asked.

"It's him," she answered dismally.

"Him who?"

"Nathan Bowman. The person I'm working with at the market now."

Annie instantly came alongside her and peeked out the window. "You get to work with *him*?" Her eyes grew wide.

"*Get* to?" What choice did she have? "Why would you even say that?"

"Why wouldn't I? He's so cute. And I like the way his hair waves out from under his hat. Oh, and he has really big shoulders that—"

"Annie!" Katie's head jerked, hearing her sister's much too detailed appraisal.

"What?" Annie shrugged a shoulder. "I am over fourteen now, remember? I know a good-looking *buwe* or man when I see one."

"Maybe. But, believe me, there needs to be more to a *buwe* than good looks. A man must be trustworthy and kind, and honest and respectful. And..." She moaned. "Easy to work with." Oh, she could go on and on. But she stopped there and began to wash her hands vigorously.

"I guess. But having good looks ain't a bad place to start, is it?" Annie chirped. "Besides, how do you know after only a few hours of being with him if he's not all those things anyway?"

Katie never understood why people said she and Annie looked alike. They may had been adopted from the same orphanage by the same wonderful couple, but that's all they had in common. They weren't blood-related at all. Yet, Katie wouldn't have minded if they had been. As it was, she'd always been entranced and even a bit envious of Annie's huge engaging smile. And now that beautiful grin of her sister's was accompanied by a know-it-all look. Surprisingly, right this minute, it seemed Annie was smarter and more mature than Katie sometimes gave her credit for.

"Well, I... I..." Katie stammered.

"Hmm. That's what I thought, big sister." Annie laughed, and even though it was at Katie's own expense, she didn't care. Whatever could offer her sister the slightest inkling of joy, she was thankful for that.

"Okay, okay. Enough of this." She turned off the water and quickly dried her hands. Then gently tugging on Annie's sleeve, she veered her away from the sink and over to the wooden island. "Can you hand me the bowl of icing, please?"

Annie continued to chuckle while doing as Katie asked. Hearing her brought a slight smile to her own face as she concentrated spreading icing over the first cupcake.

"I'm *verra* glad you baked these, Annie. I'm so ready for chocolate of any kind today." She sighed. "I'm sure you know *Mamm*'s recipe by heart now, don't you?"

No answer came and Katie looked up, only to see Annie heading out of the kitchen.

"*Schweschder*, what are you doing? I thought we were icing these together."

"Don't you want to peek out the front window and see where he's going?"

"*Nee*, I don't. Not one bit. I've seen enough of him for

one day, *danke*." She paused. "Annie, seriously. Can we forget about Nathan and get the cupcakes iced, please? He's probably down the street by now anyway."

As if on cue, the familiar ding of the registration desk bell sounded from the entryway.

"Oh, *nee, nee*." Her shoulders sagged with dismay. "Please tell me it's not him."

Taking her literally, Annie took a few steps out of the kitchen and poked her head around the corner. Turning around quickly, she scurried close and whispered, "It is him, Katie. What are you going to do?"

"Do?" Clearly, it was too late to put a plea into the prayer request box at the inn's entry asking *Gott* to have Nathan go away. So, she could forget that. "I'm going to finish icing the cupcakes," she declared. "That's what I'm going to do."

That said, before she could move, the bell pinged again.

"Don't look at me with those beseeching eyes of yours, Annie. I'm not going out there. I'm sure Mary Louise will be downstairs to take care of him any minute now."

"Thousand one, thousand two, thousand three…" her sister began to chant as her lips broke into a smile.

"It's not funny, Annie."

"I'm sorry," her sister apologized while still appearing tickled and amused. "But you should see your face, Katie. Are you wishing you were back in school again too, *schweschder*?" Annie laid a gentle hand on her shoulder.

Oh, if her sister only knew…

At this age, there were so many hopes she never stopped hoping for. So many prayers she kept asking *Gott* to hear and make true. And having the next month pass by quickly? More than ever, that was one of them.

"Hello? Anyone here?" Nathan's voice rang out.

Katie jolted at the sound. Then quickly decided to ignore it. She started to dip her knife back into the icing. At once, Annie clamped a hand over hers and looked at her with unwavering eyes. "Katie, you know Mary Louise appreciates you greeting a person when she's busy. You've done it before."

Katie groaned in response, knowing Annie was right.

Again, when had her little sister become so grown up?

And what was it about Nathan Bowman that had her behaving so childishly?

"Coming!"

A somewhat harsh voice called out to Nathan, startling him. The sound was such a contrast with the atmosphere of the inn. As soon as he'd entered the inn, he'd been heartened to see that everything about the entryway looked the same as it always had. And it had felt that way too. How many times as a young boy had he skipped up and down the L-shaped staircase next to the registration desk that led to the second floor? And until now, he'd never really appreciated how handsome the dark walnut treads over the painted white stair bases were. Or what a good job Mary Louise's late husband, Thomas, had made of the space at the bottom of the staircase, turning it into a bookcase dotted with books and small leafy plants.

Then, of course, there was the other notable item in the inn's entry. For as long as he could remember, Mary Louise had always had a wooden prayer request box sitting atop the dark maple console table there. With a slit in the top and a locked lid, there was nothing fancy about the oak piece. Even so, it had always meant so much to guests and townsfolk alike.

But that voice? Whoa. It wasn't like anything he recalled about the inn. It surely didn't fit in with the warm, welcoming, peaceful feel of the place. And it wasn't even close to Mary Louise's sweet timbre. Because sadly, the greeting hadn't come from the innkeeper he'd known all his life.

Instead, a familiar face emerged from the back of the inn and sidled up to the registration desk. Katie Troyer. He groaned inwardly and suspected she might be doing the same. She was looking about as happy to see him as he was to see her.

"Katie, what are you doing here? Are you working a second job at the inn?"

"*Nee*, not at all. Are you?"

"No." Although it was likely going to feel like another job if she was staying there too. And what a shame that would be. He'd been so looking forward to enjoying the relaxing haven the inn offered guests and even townsfolk who popped in from time to time. He was grappling with what to say next, when yet another voice called out to him.

"Nathan Bowman, is that you? *Willkumme, willkumme.*"

At the sound of Mary Louise's greeting, his heart lightened instantly. Both he and Katie turned their gazes to the staircase and watched the innkeeper skipping down the steps, like she couldn't wait to see him. But then Mary Louise had always had boundless energy in serving others. And she had a heart that reached out to everyone in Blossom Grove and beyond. Even as a young *buwe* when his family enjoyed her community benefit dinners and game-playing nights at the inn, it'd never been lost on him what a special woman she was. Even when she became widowed, her outreach to the community and guests who visited her inn only seemed to grow and flourish even more.

Without a moment's hesitation, Mary Louise came to his side and wrapped her arms around him in a motherly hug, being careful of his splinted wrist. Then she stood back, looking him up and down. "I haven't seen you forever, Nathan," the innkeeper told him. "I actually think you've grown since I last saw you."

He chuckled at that. "Nice of you to say, Mary Louise, but at twenty-six I believe my growing days are over. I didn't quite make it to six feet like my *bruder*."

"Well, however tall you are, you've always had a big spot in my heart. And I'm glad you're here now. It's been a long while."

"*Jah*, I did drop into town months ago for *Aenti* Lovina's funeral. But it was only for a *verra* quick visit and to give my regards to *Onkel* Jacob."

"I remember seeing you there, but never had the chance to talk to you," Mary Louise replied. "Well, I'm glad you're here now for a little longer visit."

"I appreciate you helping me out, Mary Louise," he said honestly. "I love my *Aenti* Sylvia, but I'm not too fond of sleeping on her love seat." He rubbed the back of his neck with his good hand. Thankfully, when the sweetest inn-keeper in all of Holmes County heard about his situation and his parents' house being rented, she'd reached out to him. She said she just had to let him know she had a room available and was running a Spring Special for four weeks. Imagine that. As if the kind woman hadn't found out from his aunt that's how long he'd be in town.

"Oh, you're more than welcome, Nathan. And I'm glad you get to stay here with your new friend Katie." Mary Louise gave his coworker a big genuine smile.

He turned his attention to Katie and tried not to wince. He'd never met someone so tightly wound. She needed to relax—so he could. "So then, you're staying here too?"

"*Jah*," she answered tersely.

"Great," he replied just as clipped.

"*Jah*, great." Katie sighed.

"Isn't it quite the coincidence with you two working to-gether and boarding here at the same time too? But then timing is everything, ain't so?" The innkeeper giggled. "With *Gott*'s timing being the best, of course."

"Of course," he replied even though he had no idea why she was bringing *Gott* into this specific circumstance.

"Well, now, Sylvia brought your duffel bag earlier, Na-than, and I put it in the first-floor bedroom. Katie, do you mind showing Nathan where that is?" she asked Katie. "And in the meantime, I'll help Annie get the table set for dinner for the four of us. I can't wait to hear all about the first day you two shared at the market."

"Dinner sounds *verra gut*, Mary Louise. But, Katie, there's no need to show me the way." He held up his hand. "I remember where that room is," he told them both. After all, Happy Endings was a quaint place with less than a handful of bedrooms. It wasn't a huge hotel.

"You're sure?" Katie asked him.

"I am, *danke*," he said.

She gave him a slight smile, appearing relieved. He was too. Yet, just as Katie and Mary Louise headed to the kitchen and he veered off toward the bedroom, something niggled at the back of his mind. It was the recollection that the owner of Happy Endings had a reputation for being quite the matchmaker. In fact, he'd always heard that she'd renamed the inn after her own happy experience with love and was determined to help others experience the same.

But even so, Mary Louise had said herself that having him and Katie staying there was a coincidence. Hadn't she? Then again, who was Annie? Hopefully, she wasn't some *maedel* Mary Louise would work to match him with. And why would Mary Louise even try? She knew he was set on leaving in a month.

Oh, well. He was probably just thinking along those lines, knowing he was going to be outnumbered by women for a while. He shook his head at himself while still feeling unsettled about the situation. Yet, just as soon as he reached his destination and opened the door to the spacious first-floor bedroom, all his paranoia went away in a flash. Seeing the full-sized panel bed covered in a navy and white star quilt with four fluffy pillows that would be awaiting him in a matter of hours, he grinned. And grinned some more.

If it turned out Mary Louise was up to something, what did it matter? For the next four weeks, he'd be sleeping comfortably and soundly. And that was worth any trouble or inconvenience, wasn't it?

Chapter Three

Katie had to laugh to herself since she couldn't cry out loud. All day long she'd been trying to keep her distance from Nathan at the market. And now, here she was in the early evening, sitting directly across the dinner table from him. *Gott, for sure and certain you're always testing me, ain't so?*

"Dinner is delicious," Nathan remarked as he looked up from his plate. "And I appreciate you making it, Mary Louise. Amish Country Casserole has always been one of my favorites."

"I'm glad you like it, Nathan. But I didn't make it by myself," Mary Louise informed him. "Katie's sister, Annie, did most of the work."

"You did?" Nathan cast his eyes on her sister.

Katie watched as Annie briefly glanced up from her dinner plate and gave a shy nod. Then right away, her sister began poking at her food once more.

Again, Katie had to laugh to herself. Earlier, Annie had been looking out the kitchen window, ogling over Nathan, and hadn't wanted to stop. Yet, ever since the four of them sat down to eat, Katie noticed her sister had barely given Nathan so much as a glance. Nor had Annie eaten much. No doubt, Annie's stomach was all in a twitter having the *cute-looking man*, as she'd described him, sitting opposite her.

Katie had to admit that even with Nathan's ruffled hair and the shadow of golden brown whiskers on his face from a day at work, he wasn't hard on the eyes. Of course, one peek at her own plate told her she hadn't devoured much either. Although her lack of appetite in his presence was due to far different reasons than Annie's.

"Well, you did a great job," Nathan complimented Annie.

Katie was sure she wasn't the only one at the table noticing her sister's cheeks turning a rosy red as a bashful smile crossed her lips. *"Danke,"* Annie replied nearly as noiselessly as a snowflake descending to the ground.

Oh, without a doubt, her younger sister was taken in by him, wasn't she? Katie's stomach tightened even more.

"I didn't know you had a sister." Nathan turned his attention to her, which she imagined made Annie glad.

"Well, I do," she answered simply.

"Why didn't you tell me?"

"Uh, maybe because you didn't ask."

His chin dipped, appearing taken aback by her clipped response. Honestly, her curtness surprised her too. But what she said was true, wasn't it?

"You're right. I didn't ask, did I?" His blue eyes turned apologetic. "Well…"

He looked from her to her sister. "It's *gut* to meet you, Annie. And I've got to tell you and Mary Louise that this is the perfect meal. Not only is it tasty, but it's something that's easy for me to eat." With a forkful of noodles, he held up his splinted wrist. "So, *danke* again," he said before taking a bite.

"How, um…did…" Annie's voice drifted.

Katie couldn't believe Annie finally mustered up the

courage to utter a word—two words—to Nathan. But then, it seemed Annie couldn't quite believe it either. Instantly, she closed her mouth and pointed to Nathan's injured wrist.

"How did I do this?" Now with an empty fork in hand, Nathan rolled over his splinted wrist, then rolled his eyes as well. "I fell. Just me being my clumsy self."

"*Jah,* Nathan did fall," Mary Louise spoke up, focusing her gaze on her and Annie. "But he wasn't being his clumsy self. That's him trying to downplay his valuable volunteer work. As it happened, Nathan fell down a ravine when he was part of a wilderness search and rescue mission."

Hearing Mary Louise's explanation, Katie noticed Annie's eyes widen. Meanwhile, hers narrowed in disbelief as she looked directly at him. "You didn't tell me that's how you injured your wrist."

"Uh, maybe because you didn't ask." He shot back the same answer she'd given him. No doubt, she had that coming. Only his delivery wasn't brusque like hers had been. His tone was teasing and so was the way a corner of his mouth curved into a slight smile.

"What is a wilderness mission?" Annie must've been over-the-top intrigued to complete a full sentence, Katie noted. "It sounds dangerous," her sister even added.

"It is, for sure." Mary Louise nodded. "And it takes a special person to volunteer for that sort of operation."

"You're being your usual kind self, Mary Louise." Nathan shook his head as if trying to shake off the compliment. "But the truth is, it's far more dangerous for the person who's lost," he continued. "Through a part of the Helping Hands Christian Ministry, we have a whole team of Amish and Mennonite men who are out there doing the search. We're working together, and we know we're there for each other. But can you imagine how frightened you'd be, being lost by yourself in the thick of a forest? Not having a clue where to go? Or which direction will take you home? I sure can't." He paused, glimpsing around the table at each of them. "I'm sorry. I start talking and get carried away sometimes."

Listening to him, goose bumps trickled up Katie's arms. She'd been trying not to get too involved in any of the conversations, but she couldn't help asking, "Did you find the person that you all were searching for?"

"We did." He nodded solemnly.

"Was he or she—?" She couldn't bring herself to say the word.

"Alive?" He seemed to know just what she was asking. "*Jah*, he was. A little beat up and dehydrated, but alive."

"May I ask who it was?" She dared to inquire further.

"It was a six-year-old boy who'd wandered far from his home."

"Oh, my!" She placed a hand over her heart while Annie gasped beside her.

"I bet his parents couldn't have thanked your group enough," Mary Louise chimed in.

"And we were all thanking *Gott* too," Nathan replied.

"Was that before or after you fell that you were thanking *Gott*?" Annie asked him with a curious smile. Obviously, her sister was quickly coming to feel more comfortable around Nathan.

"Good question, Annie." Mary Louise chuckled, turning from her sister to the only male sitting at the table.

Nathan had just started to take a bite of food and halted. "Honestly, it was both." He grinned. "When we found little Brody, we all joined in a prayer of thanks. And when I fell, I was thankful too that my wrist was all I hurt."

"*Jah*, sometimes just when we think we have a *gut* reason to be grateful, another one comes along right behind it if only we stop to notice." Mary Louise offered reflections in a way that Katie was getting accustomed to. And often looked forward to.

"That's so true," Nathan agreed. "Here I was enjoying and feeling thankful for the casserole, and then what do you know? I tasted the dinner rolls and was grateful for those too."

"They are mighty *gut*, aren't they?" Katie agreed. She hesitated, then at the last moment decided to reach for a second roll. Unfortunately, her hand met Nathan's warm touch as he sought another roll too. Instantly, she pulled back. "Actually, I've had enough to eat." She tucked her hands in her lap.

"There are plenty rolls left in the basket, dear," Mary Louise said to her. "Help yourself."

"You know *Mamm*'s recipe makes a lot at one time, Katie," Annie told her.

"I do know, but I should save room for the dessert you made, Annie."

"Dessert is from one of our *mamm*'s recipes too," Annie informed Nathan.

"Will your mother also be coming to Blossom Grove?" Nathan asked as he buttered his roll.

"*Nee*." Katie shook her head. Although her father had passed just three years earlier and her mother one year after him, it felt like forever since they'd both been gone. "She and our *daed* have been with the Lord for some time now," she said quietly.

"Ah." He laid aside the butter knife and the roll as well. "My sympathy to both of you." He glanced from her to Annie. "Is that why you decided to move here?"

Oh, if he only knew the entire reason. And what would

he think of her then? What would anyone think to know how she'd been so easily fooled by a man who claimed to love her? Yet, no one sitting around the table knew everything about her and her prior situation, did they? That even included Annie.

"My *mamm*'s parents had brought her here to Blossom Grove on a family trip when she was a young *maedel*. She always spoke so fondly of the town and even had hopes of visiting here again. So, it seemed like the perfect place for a new beginning for us."

At least that's what she kept telling herself and Annie. And what if her mother hadn't shared her cherished memories of the town? When she'd first felt pressed to flee Tuscarawas County with Annie, she wouldn't have had any idea where to go.

"And, I'm so glad you're both here in our town," Mary Louise said. "I bet Nathan is too."

Katie wasn't so sure about that. But before he could respond, Mary Louise was on to the next topic. "And how was your first day working at the market together?" She glanced between the two of them.

Katie held out her hand to Nathan for him to comment first. He was her "overseer" after all.

"It was *gut*," he answered Mary Louise. "Even though our first customer of the day was Mrs. Hochstetler."

"Oh, my." Mary Louise bit her lip, leaving Katie to *wonder* why.

"Oh, *jah*." He nodded.

"How did that go?" the innkeeper asked.

"Wunderbaar!" he exclaimed.

"Jah?" Mary Louise looked skeptical.

"All because of Katie, of course, who had Mrs. Hochstetler smiling the entire time. I've never seen anyone please

Mildred like you do, Katie." He looked from Mary Louise to her, and she was sure her cheeks were as crimson as Annie's had been. "For sure and certain, I can't," he went on to say. "The woman has never been a fan of mine."

"Why?" Annie asked, which Katie was glad about. She was wondering the same thing.

He lifted a shoulder. "Let's just say I did something disrespectful to her when I was a young *buwe*."

Katie blinked at that bit of news. Her overseer, the search and rescue volunteer, wasn't a perfect person after all?

"Oh, it wasn't as big a deal as Mildred likes to make it." Mary Louise waved a hand in the air before leaning toward Annie. "When Nathan and his friend Caleb were eleven years old or so, their *mamms* gave them money and orders to head into town to buy tomatoes. As they passed by Mrs. Hochstetler's vegetable garden, however, they thought they had a better plan. They figured why not pick some of her juicy red tomatoes and save the money for ice-cream cones in town?"

Annie giggled and, truthfully, Katie found herself somewhat amused as well. "So, what happened?" Annie asked Mary Louise. "Did the boys get in trouble?"

"As it turned out, Nathan and Caleb never even made it into town. They got caught and gave Mildred the money, paying her for the tomatoes they picked. But, she's one of those people who never forgets."

"Never," Nathan repeated. "It seems our idea wasn't so clever after all. And the moral of the story is—"

"Don't do anything wrong?" Annie interjected.

"Well, *jah*." Nathan nodded. "But also, don't get involved with anything you can't live down. Not even something like picking someone's tomatoes. Not unless you want people to still be talking and remembering about it a decade and a half later."

He chuckled at his own expense and Annie and Mary Louise joined in with him. Meanwhile, Katie felt everything inside her stiffen. She could barely feign a smile.

"That's how our town could be too, ain't so, Katie?" Annie asked her.

"Sometimes, *jah*," she replied offhandedly.

Obviously, what Nathan was saying was mostly in jest, but his words jarred her. They carried more truth than she wanted anyone to know. As it was, the dreaded fear of Annie and her being the talk of the town was just another reason she'd had them flee from Tuscarawas County. Another motive to be tucked away while starting over in the place her mother had enjoyed so long ago. After all, she criticized herself enough for the circumstance they were in. She didn't need to hear it from anyone else.

Once they had all joined in helping to clear the dinner dishes, Nathan had to wonder if Mary Louise was up to something or just being her thoughtful self. The innkeeper insisted he and Katie take a load off their feet from their busy day and rest at the dinner table while she and Annie prepared dessert dishes for the four of them.

If Mary Louise thought the time alone would have him and Katie communicating more, she was wrong. For several long minutes, the only sound to be heard between them was Katie's foot tapping on the wooden floor. Was she annoyed to be sitting alone with him? Or anxious that she wasn't assisting in the kitchen? Or possibly both?

He wasn't sure and wasn't about to ask. Instead, he fiddled with his splint, tightening it a bit, thinking how glad he'd be when he could remove it at bedtime. As he did, the rhythmic sound of Katie's tapping halted.

"Is your wrist hurting?" she asked, nodding toward his hand.

"*Nee*. Not much."

"I told you that you didn't need to help clear the dishes, Nathan," she reminded him. "I suggested that you go rest your wrist."

"I know. But I couldn't tell if you were being nice. Or if you were trying to get rid of me." He was partly teasing and more than halfway serious.

A smile twitched at her lips, one of the few directed his way throughout the whole day. "Is that even possible?" she snickered.

"Ha! Probably not." He chuckled. "I suppose we're stuck with each other, day and night. I had no idea you were staying at Happy Endings. When were you going to tell me?"

"Me tell *you*? When were you going to tell me? I think we're back to what we said earlier. You didn't ask me, and I didn't ask you."

"I guess the real question is, isn't it odd we never heard anything about us both staying here from either *Aenti* Sylvia or Mary Louise? For sure, they both knew."

"Hmm. That's true." Her forehead furrowed. "You would think it would've come up from one of them."

"I will say it is funny though," he mused. "We've found out more about each other in one hour sitting down at a meal than we did spending the entire day together at the market."

"*Jah*, but we were busy working."

Thinking back on the day, they had kept active. But hadn't part of their busyness been a way to keep avoiding each other? It had been for him. Not that he would come out and say that right now. Instead, he veered their talk in a different direction.

"You know…if you haven't already figured it out, here at the inn, we're in Mary Louise's workspace. And, I have to tell you, I've seen her in action plenty." He grinned, remembering. "Sweet as she is, she has a way of getting people to open up. So, beware if you have any secrets to hide."

He'd only meant to tease. Yet, his jesting didn't bring so much as a smile from Katie. She merely stared at him, appearing startled and tongue-tied. Come to think of it, she hadn't divulged much about herself during the dinner conversation, had she? Most topics and questions had led right back to him.

Once again, an awkwardness hovered over them. That is, until a giggle coming from Annie in the kitchen broke the silence between them.

"Your sister seems like a *verra* nice girl."

"She is," Katie answered.

"Do you have any other sisters or a brother?"

She shook her head.

"That's a lot of responsibility, taking care of someone on your own."

Acting like he hadn't said a thing, she asked, "Do you have any sisters or brothers?"

"One of each," he readily shared. "My sister, Betsy, is older and lives with her husband, Samuel, and their family in Colorado. And my brother, Moses, is younger and lives with his wife, Celia, and their *kinner* in Kentucky. Since both had babies recently, my parents are traveling the country to see their new *grossbopplin*. Not knowing that I'd be coming back, they'd already rented out their house to a family whose home is close to being built while they're out of town."

"Do your parents miss not having any of their children living here?"

Of course, they did. But he had his reasons for trying to make a life for himself elsewhere. "They stay busy," he answered simply.

"In a way, I don't understand."

"Understand what?"

"Why didn't you stay in Middlefield while you healed if your parents were gone, and their house wasn't available?"

"Are you trying to get rid of me again?"

This time his fooling did bring a slight sparkle to her eyes. "I think it's too late for that," she quipped. "At least for the next month, right?"

"Correct," he replied. "And if you really want to know, I'd been staying with the Shetler family who own the home-building business I work for. But once I got injured, I felt like more of a nuisance living there since I couldn't be on the job. Then, when I heard about what *Onkel* Jacob was going through and how *Aenti* Sylvia needed help at the market, it made sense to come back and lend a hand. The best that I can anyway." He lifted his splinted wrist. "By the way, there's been something I've been wondering about all day."

"Jah?" Tense lines instantly formed around her eyes.

"Jah. When Iva Yoder dropped that jar of relish, how did you know it was her and not her identical twin, Ida? I've known them all my life and have a hard time telling the difference."

"Oh, that." Her shoulders appeared to relax. "Iva has a mole on her left cheek, and Ida's eyebrows are thicker."

"You actually noticed those things and remembered which twin had what?" He knew he must've sounded astounded because he was.

"I'm sure my sister wrote about the twins in her little notebook." Annie must have overhead them talking as she and Mary Louise made their way to the table each carrying two dessert plates. "She writes everything in there."

"Not *everything*, Annie," Katie denied.

"The same notebook that has the color codes for the keys?" he asked.

"That's the one," Katie replied as she picked up her spoon.

For a moment, he wondered if she'd jotted down anything about him after their day together. But he readily dismissed that uneasy thought as Mary Louise set down a plate filled with a cupcake and a scoop of vanilla ice cream in front of him. "This dessert looks *wunderbaar. Danke*, Mary Louise and Annie."

"You're welcome," they both muttered.

"You know, Nathan…" Katie started as she cut into her cupcake with her spoon. "One of these days you might consider having the market offer some other freshly made desserts besides fry pies."

"Hmm. That's a thought," he replied.

It seemed Katie was back to business, and that was a good thing in his opinion. He had no intentions of thinking of them as anything more than coworkers. Even if he did notice Mary Louise's eyes shining as she watched the two of them interact.

Don't get your hopes up, Mary Louise, he wanted to tell her.

From what he knew of Katie, she was a hard worker, a caring sister and had a pretty smile that warmed a lot of people whom she spoke to. When the rare chance came along that she offered one of those smiles to him, he knew that to be true as well. But beyond being his coworker temporarily, that's as far as his interest in her went. And realizing she didn't seem too keen on sharing much of anything personal with him, he was certain that was true of her as well. Normally, that might have hurt his ego. But in this situation, their common interest in the market's success was all that mattered as far as he was concerned. Their shared goal would be plenty good enough for them to get along just fine until it was time for him to leave Blossom Grove again—which couldn't be too soon.

Chapter Four

❧

"Katie, wait up!"

Katie had done everything she could think of in order to start the day with a little time to herself outside of Nathan's presence. She'd especially wanted whatever reprieve she could get since she hadn't been able to stop Annie from yakking about him in their bedroom before falling asleep the night before. For that reason, she'd gotten up earlier than usual. She'd quickly eaten a bowl of cereal while standing guard in the kitchen. And she'd slipped out of the inn as quietly as she could. Yet somehow, Nathan was suddenly close behind her as she strode down Main Street toward the market. So near to her, that unfortunately, there was no way that she could pretend not to hear him calling out her name.

Taking a deep breath and releasing it slowly, she turned to face him. "*Guder mariye* to you," she greeted him. Oh, she was getting so good at forming a phony smile and adding a lilt to her voice when it came to her overseer.

"Same to you, Katie. And such a nice one, don't you think?"

She assumed his wide smile had everything to do with the sunshine that had broken through the clouds. Doubtful that he was that gleeful seeing her. Even so, she felt somewhat ashamed that his grin appeared truly genuine when hers hadn't been at all. After all, it was true that *Gott* had provided a beautiful start to the day for which she should be thankful.

"*Jah*, it is," she replied, giving everything around her a second look. That included Nathan. This time the smile she offered was sincere.

"The robins sure are singing today, ain't so?" He pointed to a cluster of trees behind the shop buildings.

Cocking her head, she took a moment to listen. "For sure and certain they are."

"Whenever I hear them sing, it reminds me of my *gross-mammi*."

Surprised by the sweetness of what he said, she drew her eyes to his ruggedly handsome face. "Did your grandmother have a pretty singing voice too?" she asked.

"Honestly, I'm not so sure about that. But *Gott* did give her a different kind of special talent."

Curious, she couldn't imagine what he was leading up to. "What was that?"

"She enjoyed drawing birds of all kinds, especially robins."

All at once, his reminiscing triggered memories of her own. Feeling as if she'd been punched in the pit of her stomach, her footing faltered.

"Katie, are you *oll recht*?" Nathan placed a steadying hand on her shoulder.

"*Jah*, I'm fine." But that was a lie. She wasn't fine. Not at all. Not when remembering that it hadn't been too long ago her notebook had been filled with her own sketches. Drawings of every creature that *Gott* brought close to her home. But why even share that? That had been a different time in her life. And things weren't so whimsical and quaint for her anymore. Now her new notebook was filled with practical reminders about the market and its custom-ers. The pages were also a place where she kept calculations of monies earned and dollars spent. She'd even jotted down a hopeful date of when she might be able to afford to rent a place for her and Annie to move into. "There must've been a dip in the sidewalk." She fibbed to slough off his concern.

Nathan gave a quick glance behind them, and she was sure he didn't see anything faulty in the concrete. Thankfully, he didn't say so. Instead, he was already on to the next topic, and she was grateful for that too.

"I don't believe I mentioned this before, but Abram Lytle had his own business for years."

"What kind of business?" she asked.

"He repaired buggies and bicycles. He did well and has always been well-liked by townsfolk."

"It sounds as if you may already have your mind made up about him."

"*Nee, nee.* I'm just filling you in."

That was hard to believe from the obvious excitement in Nathan's voice. But then, would it be such a bad thing if the first person they interviewed was a keeper? Then Nathan could help train him and get back to Middlefield sooner if he wanted to. A thought that made her step even lighter and in sync with his as they neared the market.

A half hour later, however, after sitting with Abram and Nathan in the market's closet-sized office, she shifted un-comfortably in her chair. Nathan appeared to notice.

"Katie, do you have any questions for Abram?" Nathan asked.

Throughout the time set aside for the interview, Nathan mostly chatted with Abram about folks in town and what was going on in the Lytle family. All the while, the older man sat back in the chair with his arms crossed over his chest, stroking his slightly graying beard from time to time. He appeared mighty comfortable as if the job was already his. That level of casualness was a far cry from what she'd experienced when Sylvia had interviewed her. And while she hated to be the one to ask the tough questions, a business was at stake, wasn't it? A business she'd grown to care about. And if it failed, she'd be out of a job as well.

"*Jah*, I do." She turned to the older man, mindful to ask as kindly as she could. "Mr. Lytle—"

"You can call me Abram."

His offer only made her feel worse. She took a deep breath. "Abram, can you say why you were late getting here this morning? Were you feeling ill maybe?"

"Oh, *nee*." He waved a dismissive hand. "I had a second cup of *kaffe* and lost track of time."

Taken aback, her mouth dropped open. "Huh!" was all she could manage to utter.

Whereas, Nathan came to Abram's defense. "Things like that happen," he replied before turning to her again. "Any other questions?"

"*Jah*, I, um…" She cleared her throat. "I'm wondering. Why do you want the job here at the market?"

"Oh, that's easy. My wife, Martha, thinks it'd be a *gut* idea. She wants to get me out of the house more. Since I sold my business, she's not used to having me around so much."

"Inter…esting," Katie coughed, practically choking on the word.

"Well, Abram," Nathan finally spoke up. "With the job here, you'd be gone from morning till it's time to go home for supper."

Katie could hardly keep her mouth shut as her eyes widened. Was Nathan really considering offering this man the job without even consulting her?

Abram looked as confused as she felt but for an altogether different reason. "I knew I'd have to be here early in the morning, but the market's been closing in the early afternoon in the past months. And has hardly been open on Saturdays."

Nathan shot her a look.

"It's true." She nodded. "At least it has been that way when I first started a few weeks ago." The hours hadn't been consistent and neither had her pay. She'd been hoping that would change when things settled down for Sylvia.

"Then the question is, Abram, would you be willing to work long hours to get the market back on its feet?" Nathan asked.

Abram glanced between them before shaking his head. "I don't know. I'm supposed to be retired. But Martha sure isn't going to like me being around all the time. So, *jah*, I guess maybe I could." Yet even as he said so, his voice rose as if questioning himself.

Feeling for him, Katie gave the man a friendly look. "Abram, can you give Nathan and me a minute? And, Nathan, may I speak to you?" She pointed toward the open door.

Nathan immediately followed her out to the deli counter beyond Abram's hearing range. She had a lot she wanted to say but wasn't sure where to start.

"Nathan, I know you'd like to get everything settled so you can leave town on time, but Abram—"

He held up a hand. "Katie, don't you worry. I'm not going to hire Abram. When I told you about him earlier, I was remembering him as a more virile and businesslike man. Even after talking to him a few minutes, I knew his heart wasn't in this. That's why I kept the conversation going about his family and friends."

"Oh." She blinked. Perhaps she'd underestimated her temporary boss.

"I just need to figure out a way to break it to him. Something that he can tell Martha."

"Well…" She dared to look into his eyes. "Maybe you could hire Abram to be a sort of repairman."

"For customers' bicycles and buggies?" His forehead creased.

"Oh, please, Nathan." She crinkled her nose at him. "You're not that stupid."

"Thanks, I think." His brows furrowed even more.

"But if money allows, Abram could do odd jobs around here. He could fix what's broken. Be the market's all-around handyman. It may not be full-time like his wife wants, but it may be what he'd like to do."

"Ah, *jah.*" Nathan gave her a knowing look. "And I know the very first job I can give him to do. When I got back to town, I noticed that from the antique mall at one end of the street to the coffee shop at the other, the front of every business appeared fresh and welcoming like spring itself. All except for *Onkel* Jacob's market. I'll tell you, Katie, it pained me to see the store look so rundown. The place really needs a new coat of paint. Not that I can do that." He lifted his splinted wrist.

"But maybe Abram can do that and more."

"You know, you're not too stupid yourself, Katie."

She started to giggle, knowing he was teasingly getting back at her. But then seeing the intense look of appreciation in his smiling blue eyes startled her. It was nothing she was used to. "We, um, should go tell Abram before customers start coming in." She began to scurry away, wanting to be out of his eyeshot. He stopped her with a hand on her shoulder. Reluctantly, she turned to face him.

"Katie, why didn't you tell me the truth?"

The truth? Her breath hitched. Did he mean the full reason she'd come to Blossom Grove? But how could he know about her past? Or know everything that had happened to her?

Heart pounding, she attempted to sound calm. "I'm not sure what you mean, Nathan."

"I'm talking about the market closing early most days."

"Oh, *jah*, that." Exhaling softly, her pulse began to slow itself.

"Can we set aside some time to talk about that?"

"Of course. The sooner the better. It was on my list to go over with you, trust me."

Trust me? Could she really say that to anyone?

As they walked back into the office to talk with Abram, she couldn't stop from wincing inwardly. Nor could she stop hearing those words reverberating in her mind. She was so weary from keeping secrets of her past. But didn't she have to in order to secure her future?

The sun was just beginning to set when Mary Louise poked her head into the inn's sitting room. And Nathan was glad she did. The raised voices between Katie and Annie coming from the dining area had been making him feel uncomfortable.

"It sounds like the sisters are bonding," his favorite innkeeper said.

"Is that what their squabbling is called?" he asked.

Katie had agreed to meet him after dinner and dishes in the small room right off the entryway. Typically, the tucked away spot couldn't have been more relaxing. Quiet and cozy with pillows on the armchairs and a braided rug gracing the floor, it was the perfect place for settling in to read or play a board game as he had as a young *buwe*. Or even to talk shop as the two of them had planned to do since they hadn't had a chance during the workday. But now with the sisters at odds in the background, he found himself doubting that was going to happen—which was fine with him. For sure, he didn't want to put any more pressure on Katie.

"Can you tell what they're arguing about?" He hadn't been able to make out anything they were saying.

"Passing by them, I got the impression Annie wanted to leave and go walking in town alone. Katie played the mom role and said no."

"Ah. I should go tell Katie that she's free to go out with Annie. She probably felt like she had to come talk with me about the market instead."

He started to get up from the armchair. Mary Louise patted her hand in a downward motion. "*Nee*, Nathan. I know you only want to help, but it's better that you sit still. Don't get in the middle of it. If Katie wants to change her plans with you, let her be the one to decide."

"Okay." He shrugged. "You're wiser about these things than I am."

"I don't know about that. But I will say, today I had Annie go with me to a quilting circle at Edna Beiler's house. The girl is delightful and tries so hard to please. But being around a bunch of women making quilts for the annual fundraiser couldn't have been *verra* enjoyable for her. There wasn't one *maedel* there her age. As it is, Annie's too old for school and too young for singings and *Rumspringa*."

"I do remember that in-between time in my life." Yet, he'd had a brother and a sister who, as annoying as they could be, were still living at home with him. Plus, growing up in Blossom Grove, he knew just about everyone in town and had plenty of friends to choose from.

"Also, as I get to know Annie more," Mary Louise continued, "I know she's fond of baking and likes quilting somewhat. But she does talk longingly about outdoor activities she used to enjoy."

"Like?"

"Softball, fishing, volleyball."

He smiled. Those were the best activities of all. The girl had it right in his opinion. "Who can blame her? I used to—"

His reminiscing halted at the sound of stomping footsteps ascending the staircase. A rather hasty closing of the second-floor bedroom door followed. He looked at Mary Louise who bit her lower lip, appearing as flummoxed as he was. Not sure what to expect next, neither of them budged an inch. Movement only came when a red-faced Katie drifted up to Mary Louise's side.

"Everything's *oll recht*," she said hoarsely. "Although I'm sure it didn't sound that way."

Normally, he might've thought her drooped shoulders and downcast eyes, along with her colorless cheeks, might be indications of a tiring day on the job. Yet, no doubt her exhausted-looking features were from even more than that. And his heart went out to her. Just the same, he didn't know what to say. He was thankful when Mary Louise spoke up in her nurturing, maternal way.

"Moving, well, living anywhere new is an adjustment. And not always an easy one." Mary Louise's comforting tone seemed to soothe Katie, prompting her to open up.

"Jah," Katie agreed, folding her arms over her chest as if giving herself a much-needed hug. "Annie's been through a lot, for sure and certain. She was adopted when she was two years old. Our *daed* went to be with the Lord right after her eleventh birthday. Then *Mamm* passed away when

Annie was twelve. And now, well…" She shook her head and straightened as if she'd suddenly caught herself sharing too much. "Uh, but anyway, sorry for the delay. I'm ready to talk about the market now, Nathan."

"Before you two get started, can I get you some tea or anything?" Mary Louise asked.

He and Katie both shook their heads.

"All right then. I'll leave you be." The innkeeper offered a tender smile prior to slipping away.

Before Katie even had a chance to come sit near him, she began getting right to the point of their meeting. "I have all the days and times the market closed early jotted down in my notebook for you to see." She reached in her apron pocket. Her hand came up empty. For a moment she seemed confused, even notably worried. Then she remembered. "Oh, that's right. I laid it on the dresser upstairs earlier. I'll go up and get it."

Just as she began to angle toward the staircase, he stopped her. "Katie, seriously, don't bother. You—we've—had a long day. Sylvia had told me that business at the market wasn't what it used to be. I suspect the irregular hours might be why. We just need to figure out how to let people know we'll be open regular hours to serve them. So, for right now, all I need from you is the answer to the same question I asked Abram. Do you want to work from open to a normal closing time like we did today?"

"*Jah*, I do. I'm definitely counting on it." The tenseness in her face slackened. She almost looked relieved. "Not only do I want to help the market make a new start because it's given me and Annie a new start too, I also need to work and make enough money for us to move into an apartment, a place of our own. We can't live at Happy Endings forever.

I sure don't imagine Mary Louise will miss having us and our drama around. She probably can't wait for us to leave."

"Don't let her hear you say that. She'd be crushed. I can tell she thinks much of you and your *schweschder.*"

He could've added that he was beginning to as well. But being that they were merely fellow workers, it was smarter that he didn't say it out loud. Or even think it to himself. "How about we get a *gut* night's sleep? Tomorrow I'll let you know how we're going to resolve the problem."

"Oh." She quirked a brow. "You don't want my help now?"

Her expression had returned to its crestfallen state. He'd only been trying to protect her. "I wasn't meaning that, I just thought…" Didn't she have enough problems on her plate? Even so, she looked so hurt he took back what he said. "What I meant to say is, we'll figure it out tomorrow."

"Gut."

"Jah, gut."

"Guti nacht, Nathan."

"Same to you, Katie."

Once again, he heard footsteps traipsing up the L-shaped staircase. But Katie's steps were lighter than Annie's had been. He found himself hoping her heart was feeling a bit less heavy too as the sound of the bedroom door closed softly behind her. After all, she was such a caring person. She cared so much for her sister. Wanted the best for his uncle's market. And was even concerned that she might be imposing on Mary Louise. That was a caring person, indeed.

Ah well, not much he could do about any of that. He sighed. And was just about to head to his own place of solitude when Mary Louise tiptoed into the sitting room.

"What do you think?" she asked.

"About the market? I told Katie we'll discuss it again tomorrow."

"*Nee*, not the market. How do you think you can help Katie with Annie?"

"Me?" What kind of question was that?

"*Jah*, you, Nathan."

"Mary Louise, I don't mean to be rude, but I'm not sure you're seeing this the right way. I can tell that Katie wants to keep things to herself and would rather not have anyone get involved."

"You mean like someone else I know?" She stared down her nose at him.

He ignored the question. "What *can* I do?"

"I'm sure you'll think of something."

"Have you?"

"Oh, well." She glanced away from him, seeming to concentrate on brushing an unseen wrinkle from the skirt of her dress. "As you know, I'm quite a busy person. I can't think of everything."

Yes, Mary Louise was truly busy. But he wasn't sure he was buying what she was saying. As far as he knew, she'd never ever been too busy to help someone.

Then again, was he overanalyzing some ulterior motive she might have? Or was she simply being her considerate self?

"Well, I don't know that I can come up with anything either."

"Promise me you'll sleep on it," she told him before bidding him good-night.

As he rambled off to his own bedroom, once again he sighed. When he came back into town, he'd been prepared to be involved in his *Onkel* Jacob's market. But to get tangled up and drawn into some virtual strangers' lives? No, he hadn't planned on that. Although he could appreciate firsthand how difficult an adjustment like moving could be—just as Mary Louise had said—he barely knew the Troyer girls.

Even so, as he got ready for bed, thoughts of fun times he'd had fishing, playing volleyball and especially softball kept streaming through his mind. Those memories were even there when he laid his head on his pillow to sleep.

With eyes closed, he saw it all. That day at school recess playing softball. Moses was on first base, and he was up to bat. The first pitch came slow and easy. He hit it right off. It went flying into the air. Moses took off running while he hustled toward first. But he was so caught up watching Moses round the bases that he tripped over his own feet before making it there.

As he began to drift off to sleep, his heart felt the same gladness and peace that he'd had watching Moses slide into home that day.

Until…the same gut-wrenching image came to mind all over again.

Because just as Moses had gotten to his feet and brushed the dust from his kneecaps, there it was once more. The wretched scar on his brother's face. The visible reminder of what he'd let happen to his younger sibling.

Jolting up in bed, Nathan worked to catch his breath. Tranquility faded quicker than a shooting star. His heart pounded wildly in his ears as he grabbed one of the extra pillows. Forcing himself to lie back down, he covered his head, trying to shut out the vision. All the while, he uttered a prayer for restfulness and forgiveness.

Chapter Five

It wasn't abnormal when Miller's closing time came around for Katie to be tired from dealing with customers and being on her feet so long. Typically, however, once her shift was over, she'd recover quickly, getting a second wind. Yet, from the way she was feeling as Nathan began shutting down everything, she wasn't so sure that would be happening this evening. She'd started out the day at work yawning. She found herself ending the day there the same way. Not only did her shoulders ache, but her legs also felt heavy. Her head throbbed too. And why wouldn't she feel that way? After her run in with Annie the evening before, she hadn't gotten much restful sleep. Lying in the twin bed next to her dear sister's, she'd tossed and turned, stewed and prayed, consumed with wanting to do what was best for Annie. Thoughts of her sister hadn't only kept her stirring for hours on end during the night, but had crossed her mind plenty throughout hours of the day too.

"Katie, I promise we'll make time tomorrow to talk about how we're going to advertise our store hours. That okay with you?" Nathan asked as he double-checked freezer doors to make sure they were tightly closed.

"*Jah*, it's fine with me," she replied. More than fine. At the moment, rustling up creative energy seemed as impossible as plotting a trip to the moon. "At least you got Abram situated today, so that's *gut*," she noted. "One step forward, as they say."

"*Jah*, but I'm sorry you got stuck doing everything by yourself for a while. I hope you didn't mind too much. I wanted to get with Abram and look over the outside of the market together, so we'd agree on what needed to be done."

"That makes perfect sense. Does that mean there are other issues besides the paint?"

He nodded. "With the exterior being wooden, there are places that need sanding and repairing. I hadn't noticed it before, but it also looked like a woodpecker was trying to make a home for itself on the far right of the building."

"The poor thing is going to have to find a new spot."

"I know. When I took Abram next door to Edward's hardware store for supplies and paint, I did notice a birdhouse there. But...we'll see. First things first."

As much as they'd been all business, she couldn't help but think how sweet it was for him to be concerned about a little bird. Maybe he truly was a rescuer at heart. *Or perhaps not*, an inner voice warned. She had been fooled before.

Wanting to shift her thoughts from the past back to the present, she changed the subject. "It was nice of Abram's grandkids to stop by to see him," she said. "They looked to be around Annie's age."

"They are," Nathan told her. "Rachel just turned fourteen, and Andrew is sixteen."

When the teens first showed up, Nathan invited them inside the store to pick out whatever treats they wanted. That was before he joined them on the sidewalk with their *grossdaddi*. Peeking out the window, she saw them all helping Abram putty and sand rough spots on the market's exterior—with Nathan using his left hand, of course. She also noticed how the teens seemed to enjoy Nathan's company as much as Annie did—once her sister had gotten comfortable with his undeniably good looks.

"Anyway, I know it all made for a disruptive day for you," Nathan continued. "You do look tired. Not tired in a bad way. But in a good way. I mean, you look *gut* but tired."

For sure and certain, she wasn't used to him bumbling so much. She held up a steady hand. "It's all in a day's work, Nathan. I'm fine."

"I do appreciate it, Katie."

"You're welcome," she replied, anxious to get out from under his gaze. Why was he being so overly nice to her?

"So, are you ready to head back to the inn?" he asked as he turned off the lights and took one last glance around. All of which was usual. What was unusual was the twinkling glimmer in his eyes when he turned to look at her. "I sure am," he added with a smile he appeared unable to contain.

She blinked, confused once again by him being so animated. Was he excited about getting back to the inn to eat the leftovers Mary Louise said she'd be serving for supper? Or was there some dessert she didn't know about? *Ach*, who knew what went on in the minds of men? She was too tired to ask.

"I'd planned to make a stop first," she told him.

"Oh." Disappointment immediately turned his smile upside down. "Anything I can help with to get the job done quicker?"

"*Nee*, not really." She knew she had to look puzzled because she was. Why was he suddenly so concerned about her comings and goings? "But, *danke* anyway. I'll be back to Happy Endings soon."

His shoulders sagged, and she couldn't imagine why. As

he went south on Main Street and she headed north, his re-action still had her wondering. That is, until she reached her destination and sauntered into Clara's Cupboard.

When she'd stopped by the store once before to do some window-shopping, she'd been delightedly overwhelmed by everything she saw. But being inside the quaint little shop was an even more mesmerizing experience. All at once, her heart dipped, thinking of her *mamm* and wishing she were by her side. How her mother would've loved browsing all the special items in Clara's shop. There were greeting cards featuring watercolor art. Packets of statio-nery and envelopes tied up in pretty bows. Mugs featur-ing scripture verses to start off the day. Faith-filled books. Recipe books. Bright-colored dish towels in every hue of spring. Handmade aprons and zippered pouches. Small baking utensils. All of it brought a smile to her face, espe-cially when her eyes landed on just what she was looking for—cookie cutters to fit the season. Wouldn't Annie love to make and decorate tulip-, butterfly-, baby chick- and bunny-shaped sugar cookies?

Right away, her mood shifted, and her weariness began to subside. Until she turned over the plastic container and saw the price on the back. Then she swallowed hard, de-bating. Hoping to spend ten dollars maximum, the pack-age was fifteen dollars plus tax. Not that the cutters weren't worth it. They were. And seeing the pleased look on her sister's face—that would be worth it too. Right?

Grasping the package, she scurried over to the checkout counter before she could change her mind.

"Anything else you'd like?" the white-haired clerk asked her. "We have some specials today." She pointed to the blackboard behind her, which featured a tempting list of items.

"There's plenty that I'd like for sure. But this will be all for now, *danke*," she said. Yet as soon as she glimpsed boxes filled with half a dozen oatmeal raisin cookies—Mary Louise's favorites—sitting at the end of the counter, she hesitated. "Er, on second thought, I'll take one of these too." She placed the cookies next to the cutters.

"All right." The woman scanned the items. "Altogether that'll be twenty-two dollars and forty-seven cents."

Her chest tightened hearing the number. Sifting through her purse for her wallet, she made a mental note to write down the expenditure in her notebook. Again, her purchases were over twice what she'd planned to spend. But she couldn't begin to tally what Mary Louise had spent on her and Annie, could she? Especially in terms of kindness and friendship. Besides that, the sweet innkeeper also made sure no one ever missed a meal. Katie didn't believe for one minute that Mary Louise continuously cooked for her shorter stay guests beyond making breakfast. Even so, she did believe Mary Louise took pleasure in seeing people enjoy her cooking. And from what she'd witnessed, Mary Louise also seemed tickled to have Annie's helping hands in the kitchen. The situation certainly eased Katie's mind, knowing Annie was safe. Once again, that alone was worth a hundred times more than a box of cookies.

With her purchases in hand, her steps felt livelier than they had all day as she headed to the inn. Yet the closer she got to Happy Endings, she heard squealing coming from the side yard—shrieking that sounded like Annie. Her heart pounded and so did her footsteps as she raced ahead. Bracing herself, she crossed in front of the inn and came to the grassy section on the other side of the two-story house. Once there, squealing wasn't the only sound to be heard. There was laughter too. In the small stretch of yard, a fun-loving softball practice was taking place. Abram's grandson Andrew was pitching. His granddaughter Rachel was playing catcher. Annie was up to bat. And Mary Louise and Nathan made up the mini outfield.

Mary Louise noticed her first, welcoming her with a huge smile from where she stood a little way to the left behind Andrew. Annie must've sensed her there. She freed her left hand from the bat she was holding and waved. Even from where Katie stood, she could see her sister's flushed face. Was that from the excitement of playing softball once again? Or because of the cute teenaged *buwe* who was pitching to her? Katie suspected it might be both. She hadn't seen Annie that lit up for quite a while.

"You made it!" Nathan called out and came running over to her.

"I'm guessing this is why you were questioning me when I left the market earlier?" she asked as soon as he reached her side. "Was this your idea?"

"Uh, yeah." He paused to scratch his chin. "You're not mad, are you?" He tilted his head, appealing to her with his deep blue eyes. A sheepish grin curved his lips. Altogether, it was a look she imagined he'd used when trying to charm his way out of trouble as a young *buwe*. Fortunately for his sake, it still worked for him as a man.

"*Nee*, I'm not mad. Just confused," she said truthfully. "How did you know Annie likes—well, loves—softball?"

"Oh, about that." He nodded toward the so-called outfield. "An innkeeper told me."

Obviously, that meant Annie had shared her likes with Mary Louise. Maybe because Mary Louise had asked Annie, seeing how lost or bored Annie seemed sometimes? Then in turn, no doubt Mary Louise had spoken to Nathan. It truly touched her to see the exuberant expression on her sister's face, her gleeful smile and crimson cheeks. Even so, knowing it had nothing to do with her, guilt stabbed at her, leaving her feeling negligent.

"Then when I met Abram's grands today," Nathan continued, "I asked if they'd like to come by for batting practice. Since they just moved back to Blossom Grove and are a little lost, they jumped at the chance. They brought their own baseball mitts and a couple of balls. And I knew Mary Louise had some equipment stored away too. It's old stuff I used to play with as a matter of fact."

"That old, huh?" She quirked a brow, causing him to chuckle.

"*Jah. Verra* old. Around your age too, I'm guessing."

Was he trying to learn more about her? It didn't matter. She ignored his comment along with his gaze, casting her eyes on the players. "You're quite the organizer."

"It was *gut* timing the way things worked out, that's all."

Hadn't Mary Louise said timing was everything?

"Where'd you stop?" Nathan glanced at the bag in her hand. "Did you find what you were looking for?"

She thought she had. Yet once again, a feeling of ineptness niggled at her, knowing it was nothing in comparison to what Nathan had done. Even more, his special gift to her sister hadn't cost a cent. How could she have been so shortsighted only trying to keep Annie happy in the kitchen?

"It's just a little something I picked up," she replied. Truly, a little something. She felt her shoulders slump, but Nathan didn't appear to notice.

"Ah, *gut*. So how about it? Want to play? Mary Louise and I can sure use your help. There's an extra mitt for you too, since I can't use one. I can't catch any ball except for grounders with my left hand. And I can barely throw with my left hand either."

"That sounds like me, and I have two *gut* hands."

He chuckled. "It all takes practice."

"And for sure and certain, I'm out of practice."

"Well, no worries. It's all just for fun. Come on."

Nathan held out his hand, inviting her. She pretended to not see it. Instead, she set the bag from Clara's Cupboard on a garden bench and made sure to follow behind him. As she did, her unease mounted. Her anxiousness had nothing to do with being rusty at softball. No, it had everything to do with all the other matters she'd grown weak and stale and out of shape with. While trying so hard to make everything right again for Annie and her, she had lost sight of so many things. If she had time to pull out her notebook, she could write out a list. Like how she was out of practice accepting help. And with trusting, even having faith in *Gott* at times. Also, she'd gone from being a fun, doting sister to continually acting like a worrisome mother hen. Nor was she accustomed to having a man be thoughtful, like Nathan had been to her sister.

"Oh, I forgot. Here's the mitt I promised you." Nathan turned to face her, pulling the broken-in glove from his rear waistband.

"*Danke*," she said, aware of her hand brushing against his as she took it from him.

"You look nervous. No need to be. Like I said before, it's just for fun." He winked at her before resuming his spot a few lengths behind the pitcher.

As she donned the mitt, she realized there was another item she could add to her notes. That would be her discomfort in dealing with a man outside of work. In spite of that, being out of practice with men didn't bother her so much. After all, over and over, she'd promised herself that no man would have a place in her future anyway.

Even so, Nathan had gone out of his way to do something nice for Annie. Because of that, coming up with a friendly way to repay him should also be on a list. And that would be friendly with a capital *F*.

Nearly another half hour into the softball practice, with the early evening temperature still in the sixties, Nathan looked around at the group assembled in Happy Ending's side yard. Somewhat boisterous and somewhat serious at times, everyone still seemed to be enjoying themselves. All of which made him smile.

Initially, he'd been somewhat reluctant to take matters into his own hands when it came to helping Annie as Mary Louise suggested—or rather, nudged him to do. Yet the more he'd thought about it, especially after meeting Abram's grandkids, he figured Annie wasn't the only one who could use some fresh air and a diversion. He could stand that himself.

He knew he was taking a risk when he'd opted to surprise Katie with his plan instead of asking her permission. But he'd really wanted to give it a chance to work out. Thankfully, even though she'd been caught off guard at first, she'd joined in.

Still and all, knowing softball was Annie's first love behind *Gott* and not necessarily Katie's, he couldn't help glimpsing to his right to check on her. As he did, he watched her tuck loose, flyaway blond hairs into her *kapp*. Then with the mitt covering her hand, she bent slightly forward with her eyes pinned on Andrew at the plate. Overall, she looked like a natural beauty. Er, a natural player, he corrected himself and shook his head. *Where had that come from?*

Yet even with that stance, there was a tenseness about her. From what he'd learned about Katie in the short time he'd known her, she seemed far more comfortable in a work environment, always smiling and more at ease, than in a social setting. No doubt, he could relate. His job in Middlefield had become his identity. Often, he too felt awkward outside of work. Like now, when she suddenly turned to look at him. She must've caught him staring at her.

"Nathan!" she yelped.

"*Jah*, what?"

"The ball," she shouted.

The ball? Clearly, he'd been so caught up in his observations he hadn't been paying attention to the smack of the bat against the ball. But now there it was, a big leather sphere sailing in the air toward him. He'd already confessed to Katie that he couldn't catch a fly with his bare left hand. Swiftly, he stepped to the right out of the way. When suddenly, a force over a hundred times heavier than a softball barreled into him. His knees buckled. He dropped to the ground. Lying flat on his back, it didn't take him long to realize that Katie had knocked him off his feet. Literally. She was lying still right next to him.

Before he and Katie could get their bearings, Mary Louise and the teens were already at the spot, surrounding them in a circle.

"Are you two *oll recht*?" Mary Louise asked, bending over them. Looking up, he saw Annie and Rachel appearing stunned with wide eyes and their hands covering their mouths. Apparently, Andrew had picked up the ball he'd hit. Clutching it in his hand, he seemed somewhat shaken.

"I'm all *gut*," he told them, not disclosing that he'd seen stars for a few seconds. Because more important than their concern for him was his for Katie. He readily turned his face toward hers. Being so close, he could see a greenish tint in her blue eyes. Something he'd never noticed before. "Are you okay?" he asked softly.

Gazing at him, her mouth opened, but no words came out. He'd seen that look before during rescue missions. Fearful thoughts began trickling through his mind. Then abruptly, she sat up. "I'm fine, everyone," she announced. "I'm fine," she repeated, looking down at him.

There were sighs all around, and he praised *Gott* silently. Rapidly getting to his feet, he held out his hand to her. This time she reached for it and held on as he helped her up.

Dusting off her skirt and straightening her *kapp*, she hardly glanced at anyone, seeming more embarrassed than hurt. "I'm sorry, Nathan." She barely eyed him as she spoke. "I hope I didn't land on your wrist."

"*Nee.* Only partially on my chest," he replied.

Her face reddened even more, making him wish he hadn't said as much.

"But that was only for a second," he assured her. "Besides, I know what you were doing. By trying to catch that ball and keep me from getting hit, Katie, you had your own best interests in mind."

Her head jerked. "*My* best interests?"

"For sure. If I was hurt, you'd have to run the market all by yourself. And I know how much you'd miss me. So much. A lot in fact." He did everything he could to tamp down the smile twitching at his lips. It must've worked because it took Katie a moment to realize he was teasing.

"Oh, you're so right, Nathan. I couldn't imagine being there without you." She dramatically placed her hands over her heart. "Why, how could I manage if you're not there to tell me how to do things I already know how to do?"

He burst out laughing and she did too. Meanwhile, no

one else had caught on to their exchange, but everyone around them did seem relieved.

"Well, I'm glad you both are fine. As for me, I'm thirsty," Mary Louise blurted. "It's time for a break and some iced tea. I'll bring drinks out to the front porch."

"Oh, and I bought a few cookies today. Let me help, Mary Louise," Katie offered.

As she took off to follow in Mary Louise's footsteps, he turned to his small group. He was impressed to see they were already gathering up the equipment without him even having to tell them. Even more, they were chatting happily as they did.

Once they all convened on the spacious wraparound porch, Mary Louise and Katie were quick to bring out the refreshments. And, the teens were quick to cheerfully relish them. That is, until minutes later when a buggy pulled up in front of the inn and a woman slipped out. He heard a slight groan come from Andrew followed by a moan from Rachel. "*Mamm*'s here. Why do we have to leave so soon?" she whimpered quietly.

"Did I come at a *gut* time?" their mother asked, standing at the base of the porch steps. Nathan would've never recognized Barbara Lytle Glick in a crowd. Not only was she at least ten years older than him, but she and her husband hadn't lived in Blossom Grove for a quite a long while.

"*Jah*, we're just having a little dessert before dinner," Mary Louise replied. "I hope you don't mind."

"As long as my teenagers are minding their manners, I'm *gut* with that."

"I'm glad to have you and your family back in town," Mary Louise told her. "I haven't seen Rachel and Andrew since they were wee big, and now they're practically all grown up, Barbara."

"It happens quickly, ain't so?"

"*Mamm*, we don't have to leave so soon, do we?" Rachel imitated Andrew's earlier groan.

"It's suppertime time for everyone. You can come back another day. And we'd welcome you all to visit us too. We're living nearby the inn. Just over on Jackson Road."

"Close to the Coblentzes?" he asked.

"As a matter of fact, we are." She narrowed her eyes at him. "Nathan, I can't believe it. It's really you. Isn't it?" She chuckled. "Talk about all grown up. Are you married now? To each other?" Barbara wagged a finger in the air between him and Katie. In response, Katie shook her head so vehemently that it shook him too. He knew they weren't at all interested in each other in that way. But her reaction was a bit overboard. Hadn't they just shared a good laugh together?

"*Nee, nee,* not married," he answered.

"Well, one of these days," she said before turning to Katie. "I'm sorry, but I'm having a hard time remembering your name."

"That's because I'm new here." Katie's shoulders straightened as she graced Barbara with a smile. "I'm Katie Troyer, and that's my *schweschder*, Annie." She pointed to where Annie was talking to Rachel and sipping on her tea.

"Katie. Yes. You're the one working at Miller's Market. *Daed* told me all about you. He'd heard you moved here from Tuscarawas County. I used to know someone from there who would visit Blossom Grove from time to time. She was a friend of my cousin. Her name was… Oh, it was…"

Nathan watched Barbara frown while casually tapping her lip with her forefinger. Meanwhile, Katie froze like twelve-year-old Karl Keim had the other day when Nathan caught him trying to pocket a candy bar at the market. Yet, he knew why Karl behaved the way he had. For the life of him, he didn't understand why Katie seemed disturbed by a simple friendly discussion.

"Hmm. I can't recall her name," Barbara finally said. As she waved a dismissive hand, he noticed Katie's shoulders relax some. "Anyway," Barbara continued, "thank you for having Andrew and Rachel come by today."

"It was Nathan's idea," Mary Louise said.

"Not really. It all started with Mary Louise." He smiled at the innkeeper, giving praise where praise was due.

"Many things in this town do start with her from what I recall." He knew Barbara was referring to Mary Louise's matchmaking reputation as she glanced between him and Katie. "Be careful you two," she warned playfully with a giggle. "All right, Andrew, Rachel, it's time to get going."

After piling into the buggy, thank-yous and goodbyes were shouted back and forth. As they pulled away, Annie sighed so loudly that Katie stopped from setting more empty glasses onto the tray. Mary Louise paused in picking up discarded napkins. And he halted from gathering up the mitts and bats. Instead, they all turned to look at the widely grinning girl.

"That was the best day ever!" she exclaimed. "Mary Louise, *danke* for letting us all play here today. And, Nathan, thank you for thinking to bring Rachel and Andrew here."

"It was fun for me too, although I wasn't much help in the outfield. Thankfully, you had your sister and Mary Louise to do that."

"*Jah*, but you made it all happen." Her eyes glistened as she spoke to him. "You're a *verra* nice man. What you did is nicer than anything Katie's husband ever did for me when he was alive. Maybe even nicer than how he was with Katie."

The sound of glass clinking resonated in the air. He looked over to see a shocked Katie trying to right the tray she held in her hands. Her mouth gaped. The same was true of Mary Louise who seemed as speechless as he was.

Finally, he replied to Annie. "Young lady, aren't you hungry after using up all your energy out there? You need to help Mary Louise get the leftovers heated up before I get to them."

"You're right." Annie giggled.

As Mary Louise led Annie inside, he heard Katie sigh. He wasn't surprised that she refrained from looking at him. From all that had been exposed, he was sure she was afraid of questions. And though he had plenty of them, his heart instantly turned sympathetic, it wasn't his business to ask or say a thing. So he didn't. He couldn't do anything about anyone's past, not even his own. Instead, he continued to gather up the baseball equipment as if nothing had ever happened. But before she headed into the inn, he sensed her pause. She finally turned to look at him. Not a word came from her lips. But in the silence that hung between them, he witnessed something that heartened him. Because there it was. A glimpse of unmistakable gratitude glimmering in her eyes.

Chapter Six

The next day, an early morning quiet filled the inn as Katie snuck out of the bedroom where Annie was still sleeping and tiptoed lightly down the staircase. Creeping toward the kitchen, she padded softly to the back door. The wooden-framed door creaked as she opened it, causing her to momentarily freeze. Then, not waiting to look around to see if anyone was close enough to notice, she hurriedly slipped out to the garden.

As soon as she settled onto the garden bench, she let go of the breath she'd been holding. Even so, there was still a heaviness in her chest. Trying to feel more at ease, she focused her eyes on hints of the approaching sunrise. Layers of pink and golden tints were already visible, stretched like strips of taffy across the sky. Yet with such an aching heart, she could hardly enjoy the awesome beauty as she had once upon a time. Instead, with every minute that passed she searched the sky, wondering if the pain she felt would ever go away. It was always there to some degree because of all the ways that Jonathan Lantz had used her. But hearing Annie mention him the night before had reawakened the hurt all over again.

How could she have been so conned by him? How could she have been so deceived?

A chill coursed through her. Even though it was from within, she wrapped her sweater more tightly around her chest as if that could make it go away. Suddenly, seemingly out of nowhere, Mary Louise's warm voice greeted her. Even as gentle as it was, she startled. And gasped. She hadn't even heard the sweet woman's footsteps. She'd been too busy, attuned to the questions plaguing her soul.

"I'm sorry. I didn't mean to sneak up on you," Mary Louise apologized. "I thought you may like some tea."

"Why, uh, *jah. Danke*," she mumbled.

She took the mug Mary Louise offered to her. As she did, seeing that Mary Louise had a mug of her own, she scooted over on the bench.

"Would you like to sit down?" She felt awkward even asking. After all, she was encroaching on Mary Louise's territory. Namely, the exact spot where she'd get a peek at Mary Louise sitting and reading her Bible most mornings.

"Only if you're in the mood for company," Mary Louise replied.

"I would like that a lot." Katie meant what she said sincerely. Not only would Mary Louise's presence keep her mind in the present but being around the woman was a comfort itself. Her own parents had been closer to a grandparent's age when she was a young child, which hadn't mattered a bit. They'd taken plenty good care of her and Annie even so. But the older she got, her parents did too. Roles reversed, and it had been her turn to take care of them. Whereas, Mary Louise was as doting and warmhearted as any good mother would be and was likely only double Katie's age.

"The spring blooms are sure popping up quickly," Katie noted, trying to make light conversation. "They're lovely."

"They are, aren't they? And right over there—" Mary

Louise pointed to an open area of the garden "—that's where the celery plants will go."

"You mean all those seedlings you've been growing indoors?"

"Oh, yes. Those special little starter plants." Mary Louise nodded enthusiastically. "You can't plant them outside too early or too late. But since it's been two weeks since the last frost, it's time. I'm planning a planting party on Saturday. I hope you'll join in. It'll all be happening right after the market closes that day. So, you can help if you wish."

"Sure, I'll try to," she said hesitantly, uncertain as to what a celery *planting party* entailed. Yet, the way Mary Louise's eyes shone as she spoke about the vegetable did make her wonder. "My parents never planted celery. I suppose I never truly understood why it's important to so many Amish folks."

"Oh, there's definitely some lore attached to it. But I can only tell you what I think and why I grow it."

"And why is that?" Katie took a drink of tea.

"Because I think it's a lot like love."

Katie had been poised to listen, sipping her tea. But hearing that she coughed on the liquid. "Celery?"

Mary Louise's delightful giggle filled the air. "I know that's surprising. But I can't help but feel that way. It reminds me of love—true love, I mean. Celery is easy to get started indoors, tucking a seed in a small container of dirt. Like dipping your toes into a relationship with someone. But like love, to grow it into something more is a work of heart. You have to protect it and be aware of things that may harm it. In the case of celery, that means things like bad frosty weather. And even once it's transplanted outdoors, like love, you can't just let it be." She shook her head. "No, to keep growing it into something more, you have to give it more soil, more water, more of your time. Just like you need to keep nurturing a relationship, allowing hearts to grow deeper in love. And then, before you know it, so often that love goes on to bless others." She sighed.

When Mary Louise had first begun explaining herself, Katie somewhat snubbed the idea mentally. Yet now, she'd been swayed and was even thinking the comparison was a clever one.

"Maybe that's why it shows up at wedding receptions in creamy casseroles," she said, "to nourish people like love is supposed to." *Supposed to,* being the words that stuck in her mind.

"And with stalks tied up in a bow to be used as table toppers at the receptions, it's like how love decorates our lives," Mary Louise added.

Katie had to chuckle. "Mary Louise, I don't think I'll ever look at a piece of celery the same way again."

"You'll help plant on Saturday then?" Mary Louise asked.

Although she'd never experienced the kind of love with a man that Mary Louise spoke of, and never intended to, planting celery now sounded almost enjoyable. "Of course, I will."

They both settled back on the bench, enjoying their silence together and the sight of the rising sun. Squirrels scampered around the garden. Birds twittered from their perched spots at birdfeeders. Watching, Katie saw all of it as signals that the day was beginning. That meant she needed to get going to her job too, where she had to face Nathan.

As if it hadn't been enough to knock him off his feet and tumble next to him, how embarrassed she'd been because of what Annie had said to him. And yet…a vision of his kind expression crossed her mind. Truly, he couldn't have been more respectful about all of it, not questioning her at all. For that, she was most appreciative, and had yet another reason to do something nice in return. Whatever that might be.

She glanced into the cloudless sky and sighed. Then she was about to get up and get started, when Mary Louise's voice stopped her.

"Katie," she said her name gently, "I obviously don't know the relationship you had with your husband, but I hope and pray that any grief you feel will become less and less with each sunrise."

Katie had just begun to feel collected and calm. Now her stomach knotted. Her shoulders stiffened. For anyone else, that may have been an endearing sentiment and wonderful to hear. But for her? How could she mourn a person she never really knew? As it was, she hadn't wasted any time reverting back to her maiden name.

Afraid that Mary Louise might ask more about the man she'd been married to for two years, she quickly switched the subject.

"How long were you and your husband married, Mary Louise?" she asked.

"Oh, Thomas?" Even just saying his name, Katie could see the gleam glowing in Mary Louise's eyes. "We were married in our early twenties and were blessed to enjoy our twenty-fifth anniversary together. And then—it's been four years now—we went to bed one night. As was our custom, we kissed each other good-night and rolled over to opposite sides of our bed. A few hours later, I was awakened by his body jerking."

"His heart?" Katie winced.

"*Jah*, and his heart had been such a *verra gut* one too," Mary Louise said wistfully. "My Thomas was the most loving, faithful man I ever knew. Every day I thank the Lord for giving me such a *wunderbaar* man to love for as long as He did."

"I'm so sorry," Katie told her. She couldn't imagine loving a man like that or how difficult it must be to lose him. What she'd gone through was difficult but in an entirely different way.

"*Danke*, Katie. Like you," she said in a hushed voice, "I never had any children. But how I would've loved to have *kinner*! A little *buwe* with Thomas's crooked smile. Or a *dochder* with his deep brown eyes. But I never was able to have children. I suppose *Gott* thought that best too."

"It seems you've made it a point to serve *Gott*'s children." And from what Katie had observed in her short time in Blossom Grove, Mary Louise stayed busy at it. "You knit blankets for newborn *bopplis*, bring meals to sick folks. You host quilting bees, and I've heard about your community get togethers at the inn. All that, while being a partner in the town's thrift shop ministry."

"Oh, the people in Blossom Grove are dear to me. They've helped me much too." Mary Louise paused. "Speaking of this town, Katie, do you remember how old you were when your *mamm* told you about her visit here?"

It was odd how she could still see how her mother's eyes lit up, speaking of Blossom Grove. But it was hard to recall her age when hearing about it. "Maybe ten years old?"

"Had you ever thought about coming to Blossom Grove until recently?"

"Honestly, not really. I hadn't remembered about it until—" She caught herself. "Why do you ask?"

"I got to thinking about you last night and thought that was the case, but I wasn't sure. Oh, Katie, doesn't it just make you marvel about our *Gott* all over again?"

Katie narrowed her eyes. "I'm sorry, Mary Louise, I don't understand."

"Well, even back when your *mamm*'s parents brought her to Blossom Grove, before you were even born, *Gott* already knew you'd be here now. And I don't doubt that while you don't remember how old you were when your *mamm* told you about this town, that He's never forgotten the exact second that it happened. And again, He knew then that you'd be coming to start a new life here. He's always been with you and always will be, Katie."

Mary Louise sighed while Katie felt everything inside her wrestling. If that were so, then why hadn't He protected her? Why had He let her go through all that she had to get here? She wanted to shout up to the sky.

Where were You then, Lord?

She started to take a sip of tea to try to calm herself and those disturbing thoughts. Thoughts she guiltily knew were irreverent. Sadly, like her heart at that moment, the tea had lost its warmth.

"Katie, we don't have to talk about work if there's something else on your mind."

Nathan had hoped they'd have time during the day to discuss what to do about displaying store hours as they'd planned. But with interruptions from Abram, setting up interviews and getting in a service man to fix one of the freezer compartments, that had never happened. Plus, at one point, Katie had been busy helping an *Englisch* mom get a sucker unstuck from her daughter's brown curls. That unusual event had caused customers to back up at the checkout counter.

Finally, after locking the front door, he had scooted two stools up to that same counter. Now sitting with her elbow propped on the plywood surface, and her head in her hand, those oval-shaped eyes he'd been noticing too much lately appeared to have drifted a million miles away.

"Did you say something?" She looked at him.

All day Nathan had noticed she'd seemed distracted, and he couldn't help wondering if it was because of what her sister had revealed last evening. She was a widow. Why didn't she mention it? Was her grief too raw? All day, he'd tried to think of ways to express his sympathy, but he had the strong impression she preferred not to talk about it. Even so, he tried again.

"If there's something you'd like to talk about besides work, we can."

"Why would we do that?" Her brows furrowed. "The reason we stayed after hours is to talk about the market."

"*Verra* true. But you never answered me before when I made a suggestion. Does that mean my idea is boring to you?" he questioned her.

"Um, *jah*, maybe just a little." Lifting her head, she held her thumb and forefinger in the air, leaving about a half inch of space between them. Then she bit her lip as if sorry she'd been so honest.

Flummoxed, he crossed his arms over his chest. "You don't agree that it'd be *gut* to get a new sign in the window showing the hours? Maybe with bright red lettering?"

"It's a start." Her left shoulder lifted. "But, I'm not sure how quick people will be to pay attention to that. No one is noticing it now, right? You said we're still getting less late afternoon traffic than the market used to when the hours hadn't been fluctuating."

He knew she was right, but what then? "And do you have a better idea? If you do, I'm ready to listen."

She sat up straight. "Are you? Because you seem set that this is the answer, and I know whatever you say goes."

He frowned at her. She really felt that way? "When have I ever not listened to you?"

"Uh, like the other day when I told you I didn't think the freezer compartment was getting cold enough and you waved me off. And then yesterday when I mentioned the dumpster wasn't closing all the way and I thought raccoons were—"

He held up a hand, stopping her. "Okay, okay. But that doesn't mean I don't respect your opinion. I believe you have lots of *gut* ideas."

While a smile twitched at her lips, she eyed him skeptically.

"You do," he said emphatically.

"Then here's one of them for you. How about a chalkboard?"

"A chalkboard?" He blinked. Did he hear her right?

"*Jah*, when I was at Clara's Cupboard, they have a blackboard over the cash register area listing their specials. And so, it got me to thinking—"

"How could a blackboard inside get customers to come in from the outside?"

"If you'd stop interrupting me, I could tell you."

"I'm sorry."

"You're right. It wouldn't. Although we could have a blackboard inside listing specials or featuring Scripture or happy birthday messages or—"

Once she got started, she never stopped, did she? He gave her a blank stare, which she appeared to notice.

"I'm getting carried away, aren't I?" she said. "Look, can you get the keys?"

The keys? He was confounded once more but was ready

to comply. No need to start another rift between them. Grabbing the key chain from the drawer next to the cash register, he wrapped his fist around it. "Got 'em."

"Gut." Katie jumped down from the stool and crooked her finger. "Follow me, please."

He did as he was instructed as she led the way to the small storage room at the back of the market. However, fumbling with the keys once again, he had no clue which one would unlock the door.

"It's the purple-covered key," she informed him.

"Purple for storage?" He quirked a brow. When it came to her color-coding, that didn't make sense.

"Not exactly. It's purple for extra 'plus' stuff. *P* and *p*. I know it's a stretch."

He chuckled. "It's better than what I would've come up with."

He opened the door, and they both walked inside. As soon as he pulled on the string to turn on the overhead fluorescent light, he immediately saw exactly what Katie was thinking of. Leaning against one of the walls, there sat a wood A-frame sidewalk chalkboard, complete with a baggie of colored chalk taped to the top of it.

"You're a genius," he exclaimed.

Laughter bubbled out of her, and he was surprised how glad it made him feel. "I'll remember you said that," she told him, "since I'll probably never hear it again. And just so you know, this genius will be the one doing the printing on the board. My writing is way better than yours."

"You mean it's legible?" he quipped.

She chuckled again. "Exactly."

With that, he brought the signage board out of the closet, carrying it to the space opposite the checkout counter. The moment he had it set up, Katie was already at his side with a wet towel washing the dust from every inch of it. Once the blackboard dried, she pulled chalk from the bag and went to work.

As she did, he stood back watching, amazed. Her writing wasn't simply legible, it was full of artistic flair.

"'Stop in. We're happy to serve you,'" he read once she had finished. "'Open Monday through Friday 8 to 6, Saturdays 8 to 2, Sundays—have a blessed day!' It's perfect, Katie, perfect. And the way you wrote it—who knew displaying hours for the market could be so engaging and welcoming?" he blabbered on. "It's beautiful."

"Oh, one more thing." Grabbing several more pieces of chalk, she turned back to the board. After a few minutes of sketching, she stepped aside for him to see. At the top of each side of the chalkboard, orange-breasted robins heralded the message Katie had so creatively written there. "That's for you and your *grossmammi*," she said.

The sight of the hand-drawn birds instantly took him back to special times with his *grossmammi*. He was so completely touched by Katie's thoughtfulness that it took a moment before he could speak. "You remembered."

"Birds are some of my favorites to draw too," she admitted, placing the chalk pieces back into the baggie.

"You mean you can draw more?" His imagination began to take off. "Cows when we're running milk specials? Rabbits advertising packages of buy-one-get-one-free carrots?"

She laughed. "*Jah*, and I can draw goats, honeybees, squirrels, horses too. Most anything you'd find in a backyard."

"So, no giraffes or zebras?"

"*Nee*, I've never seen one of those up close."

He stood back, glancing at the blackboard again. "I can't wait to put this out on the sidewalk tomorrow, Katie." He looked up at her, overcome by her pleased but humble smile. "You're—" He caught himself. "This sign is *wunderbaar*. And to thank you, how about dinner on me?"

"Oh, Nathan…" She shook her head. "I don't know."

They both knew Mary Louise wasn't cooking for the evening. Earlier, she and Annie had stopped in after delivering cookies and a baby blanket to the Franz family to say that they'd been invited to the Glicks for dinner. Even so, Katie suddenly looked cautious of him.

"Maybe just some pizza?" he suggested. That sounded way less formal.

"Pizza?" Her expression brightened some. "All right. But I'm going to pay my own way," she insisted.

"How about I pay for dinner, and you pay for dessert?"

Once they agreed on their terms for the evening, they arrived at Bruno's Pizza ten minutes later. Nathan couldn't believe the crowd. It may as well have been a Friday evening. Every table was full. But not so full that he didn't instantly notice a couple that he knew. His chest immediately tightened when he spotted them, Sarah Fisher and her husband, Levi—his former best friend—with their *boppli* in the far corner. Instantly thrown off-kilter, he wasn't prepared to deal with them.

"Do you mind if we eat outside?" he asked Katie, crossing his fingers she'd say yes.

"Please," she said, gazing at the crowd. "Let's get the pizza to go."

Just as he'd remembered, the parlor's outdoor setup was a much better option. Settling into opposite sides of one of the picnic tables there, they were warmed by the fire burning in the round stone pit.

He was the first to look up after they'd bowed their heads to say grace. Oddly, he found himself thankful to be sitting across from Katie instead of the *maedel* inside whom he'd once loved.

"Are you sure this is okay with you?" he asked politely, watching her sit up and timidly tug a slice of pizza from the box.

"Absolutely," she assured him, placing the slice on her paper plate. "I'm warm. The pizza's hot. Our sodas are cold. And it's way quieter and peaceful out here."

"Simple as that, huh?"

"Jah." She started to take a bite, but then hesitated. "Are you *oll recht*? For a minute there inside, you looked like you'd lost your appetite."

"Eh, I'm fine. Sometimes a memory hits you from out of nowhere, if you know what I mean."

"Ha. I wish I didn't." She sounded just as elusive as he did, and he was glad.

"Well, I'm thankful that knowing how to draw those robins was still in your memory bank." He tried to make light of their commiserating. "Now you'll have to be drawing cows and rabbits for me too."

She laughed. "Well, drawing those robins like you'd mentioned your *grossmammi* did was my small attempt to thank you for organizing the softball practice for Annie. It was *verra* kind of you, Nathan. And honestly, I have to say it did feel *gut* to be drawing again today. I haven't had the inclination recently or the time."

"I know I don't say it, Katie, but I really do appreciate everything you do around the market. Even my *Aenti* Lovina hardly ever ran the meat slicer."

"Trust me, the job at the market is far easier compared to what I used to do. I managed and took care of a house, animals and an acre of land all by myself for the past couple of years." Seeming to realize she'd already said more than she meant to, she reached for her soda and took small sips.

"Your husband didn't help?"

"He was... It's a long story." She wiped self-consciously at her lips with her napkin almost as if swiping away any emotion she was feeling. Just like the evening before, he got the impression she didn't want to share more about that relationship. And while he had to respect her wishes, it wasn't easy to do. The more he was getting to know her, the more his heart went out to her regarding her situation. Yet, as much as he wished to express his sympathy, how could he with the closed off way she responded? He didn't feel comfortable doing so, and he surely didn't want to open a wound. Maybe her husband had had a terminal illness or some other sad issue that he couldn't even imagine. Besides, perhaps it didn't matter anyway. They'd only be around each other for three more weeks with nothing long term expected of one another.

"How about you? Is the market easier than your job in Middlefield?" she asked before taking up her slice of pizza again.

"Good question." He tilted his head. "I'd say my job in Middlefield is more physical. And for me, the market is less physical, but I feel it more. Inside, I mean." Oh, that didn't sound very masculine, did it? She gazed at him curiously. "What I mean is," he continued, "it was my first job. I worked there as a young *buwe* and then as a young man. Even then I realized the market my great *onkel* and *aenti* had built was such a great part of the community. Not just because they sold goods people needed, but they also saw to those in need. Giving to the food pantry. Providing food for families going through tough times. So, I wanted to help get it back on its feet."

"Before you go back home to Middlefield you mean?" she asked.

Home. When was the last time any place felt like home to him? And the girl he'd seen again inside Bruno's wasn't the only reason for him feeling that way.

He purposefully ignored the question.

"Hey, have you been to Daisy's Dairy Whip for ice cream yet?" he asked.

"Nee." Katie shook her head.

"Then I'd say you're in for a treat."

"Really?" One side of her mouth curved into a smile. "Because I'd say you're in for a treat since I'm the one buying."

He was on the cusp of chuckling. But then as he looked up at her, what he noticed going on behind her rattled him. A young *Englischer* boy was getting close to the firepit. Far too close. Instantly, his pulse quickened. Without a moment's hesitation, he jumped up from the table. He began to sprint toward the child. Before he got there, the boy's mother darted toward her son, lifting him up into her arms.

Silently praising *Gott* the mother had been watchful and swift, Nathan's heart still sank for the thousandth time. If only he'd done the same for his brother, Moses. Even after all the years that had passed, he had to wonder. When would the feeling of guilt ever go away?

Chapter Seven

"Will Mary Louise be upset that we're not on time for her celery planting party? I hope she doesn't wait on us."

After leaving the market, as Katie attempted to walk briskly toward the inn, she gave Nathan a cursory glance. Yet, it was enough to see there were no lines of concern etching his forehead or any tightening of his jaw. His blue eyes were bright; his broad shoulders were slack. Obviously, he was far more relaxed than she was about being late for Mary Louise's Saturday gathering.

Yet as it had turned out, their delay couldn't be helped. Even more customers had dropped into the market than they were accustomed to. Many remarked how they'd noticed the fresh new paint outside, a job that Abram had finished up the day before. Even more customers commented on how they'd been drawn in by the welcoming sidewalk sign for which Nathan gave her all the credit. She'd found herself flushing from his flattery—and from the busyness too, of course. But while it was all well and wonderful that there were more shoppers to attend to, that meant more cleaning up after closing time. Given that, even though they'd shut the market's door at two o'clock, now it was after three.

"Katie, slow down," Nathan replied in response to her stewing out loud. Then he stopped altogether, causing her to halt as well. Laying a gentle hand on her arm, he spoke softly. "You really need to calm down. There's no need to rush. We're not midwives, hurrying to deliver a baby. We're planting celery at Happy Endings Inn."

"But it's so important to Mary Louise."

"I know it is. But first of all, when do you ever see Mary Louise get upset? And secondly, her goal is for everyone to enjoy themselves. There will be plenty of people there already. She wouldn't want you to be stressed by this."

And yet even before today, in some ways she'd already been feeling distraught about the event. True, it had been interesting and somewhat amusing to hear Mary Louise's view on celery the other morning and how she likened it to love. But when it came right down to it, the issue of love wasn't dear to her like it was for Mary Louise. In fact, the topic hurt her heart immensely, with a throbbing intensity. Even more, when was the last time she'd been to a social get-together like the one Mary Louise had described? That alone was anxiety-inducing.

"So, does that mean you've been to one of these parties before?" She stared into his eyes.

"It's been years, but *jah*. I was there because of my sister."

"Hmm." That didn't make one ounce of sense to her. But she'd found that sometimes not having grown up in Blossom Grove, there were things that didn't quite jibe. Not that it was anything awful. She figured the town had its own peculiarities just like she had hers.

"Hey." He touched her shoulder lightly, interrupting her thoughts. "You've already put in a hard day's work. It's time to take it easy now. Okay?"

She nodded. Yet, she didn't know if she could manage to do that, given the situation. But she'd try anyway.

"All right. Let's go then," he said, stretching out his splinted hand to usher her forward.

They walked at an easygoing pace. Once again, as he'd done earlier in the week, he began to point out various birds. It led her to do the same, and even had her laughing when he attempted to mimic their chirps and tweets. No doubt as a result of his silliness, she could feel herself beginning to unwind. That is, until they reached the inn.

At least thirty people filled Mary Louise's backyard and garden area, mostly Amish but *Englischers* as well. A few of the women did look familiar to her from their visits to the market. Even so, she'd never seen them with their better halves. In fact, the way people were standing or milling around together, it appeared everyone was there with a partner.

The scene was worse than she'd imagined. Seeing that, she swallowed hard. "Um… I don't think I fit in here," she stammered.

"You mean all the couples?"

"*Jah, jah.* All the couples."

While her stomach churned, Nathan's eyes held a sympathetic gleam. "I'm sorry. I probably should have said something earlier. I guess you've never heard that Blossom Grove folks think of Mary Louise as a matchmaker."

"A what?" She shot Nathan a puzzled look.

"You heard me right."

"I just never thought of a matchmaker as being a real person. I figured it was like a fairy. Something folks made up."

He laughed. "Not in this town. That's why I was at one of these parties years ago like I said before. I was only going to drop off my sister, Betsy, there, and Mary Louise invited me to stay and have a bite to eat. Mary Louise is the one who brought Betsy and her husband, Samuel, together. Samuel was the son of one of Mary Louise's close friends."

"So…are you saying these are couples that Mary Louise got started?"

"Mostly. Some are invited to the planting to celebrate their union. And then others are here because she's in the beginning process of getting them to know each other better."

"Oh, my. And, here you and I were also invited." She frowned. Her chest tightened even more.

"But that's different because—"

Before Nathan could say another word, she jumped in. "*Jah*, it's different because we—you and me—" she pointed a finger at him before tapping the same finger into her sternum "—we're not anything together, Nathan. Not a couple. Not a pair." She waved her entire hand in the air, as if erasing the idea completely. Then seeing his head jerk, she realized how forceful and rude she'd been.

She hadn't meant to sound so negative or to harm his ego in any way. Especially because while they did have their bouts and disagreements each day, they were becoming friends—to some extent. After spending so much time together, how couldn't they? "Um, what I mean to say is, we're just friends, right?"

Nathan stared at her wide-eyed. She wasn't sure what he was thinking. Was he taken aback by her ranting, hurt by what she'd said or thankful she'd finally shut her mouth?

He cleared his throat. "Are you finished?" Obviously, he'd been thinking the latter.

"*Jah*, sorry." She dipped her head.

"*Gut*, because if you would've let me finish my sentence, it may have calmed your fears. What I was going to say is, we're guests here at the inn. Why else would we have been invited?"

"You've got to be right. We're guests and Mary Louise didn't want us to feel left out."

"Exactly."

Instantly, relief washed over her. Once more, Nathan had subdued her anxiousness. She started to tell him how he really was a rescuer. But thinking that was true was one thing. Saying it out loud seemed a bit too serious. Instead, she decided to simply try to enjoy the relaxed feeling settling over her. That lasted about two minutes until moving forward, her eyes landed on something in the crowd that disturbed her. Immediately, her footsteps came to a stop. Nathan followed suit.

"What's Annie doing?" She pointed to the edge of the celery garden where her sister was kneeling, digging in the earth.

"It looks like she's getting ready to plant celery." Nathan half chuckled.

"But why is Andrew kneeling right next to her?"

"Apparently, he's planting celery too."

"But so close?"

"The plants are generally about a foot apart, Katie."

"And that's close wouldn't you say?"

"For the plants or for Annie and Andrew?" Nathan crooked a smile.

After the teens finished patting the soil around their plants, they rose at the same time. Katie noticed the same giddy look on her sister's face that she'd seen during the softball practice nights before. She groaned.

"And where's Rachel?" she asked more to herself than to Nathan.

Even so, he answered. "She's right over there." He inclined his head to the right where she saw Rachel handing an *Englischer* couple glasses of tea. "Maybe Mary Louise asked the Glick kids to come help and keep Annie company. But as it turns out, maybe it's not as simple as that."

"What do you mean?"

"Well, Mary Louise typically doesn't go matching teenagers," Nathan informed her. "So, I'm not suggesting that. But think about it. No sixteen-year-old *buwe* comes to a celery planting party unless they're interested in something more than, well, celery." He chuckled.

Meanwhile, she groaned again. "Oh, no." For Annie's sake, she wished she could laugh off a possible teen crush and think it was cute. And, after all, Andrew seemed to be a nice boy. Even so, unfortunately and involuntarily, her every limb stiffened at the thought. Instantly, Nathan noticed.

"There you go getting upset again, Katie," he said. Even after just a week of being around each other, he seemed to be reading her body language quickly and accurately. "Every young *maedel* and *buwe* gets a crush on someone. An innocent little crush isn't that awful, is it? And who can blame Andrew if that's what's happening?" He glanced at the pair and then back at her. "Attractiveness runs in your family. Annie is pretty like her *schweschder.*"

Katie figured he must've suddenly caught what he'd said. Right away, he began to apologize. "I'm sorry if that was too forward, Katie. I didn't mean for it to be. It was just an observation. A *friendly* observation."

"Don't be sorry, Nathan. People say things like that all the time, and it's sweet," she assured him. "But it's funny in a way too. I don't know why I'm telling you this because I don't tell many people, but I was eight when our parents adopted me."

"You weren't adopted until you were eight?"

"*Nee.* I saw plenty of other *kinner* leave the orphanage. I suppose *Gott* was waiting for my perfect parents to come along, and they did. Four years later, they brought Annie home from the same agency. Even so, we're not blood related at all."

"Well, your parents did *gut*. You two are as pretty on the inside as on the outside. And you're quite the big sister, Katie. The way you love Annie and provide for her makes you more tight-knit than many birth sisters I know."

And that's exactly why she was going to do everything she could to protect her sister. She wasn't about to let Annie get her heart broken. There was already enough hurt and damage that had taken place due to her own gullibility. She'd tried hard to hide all that she could. There was no reason Annie needed to know even half of it.

Nathan was of the same mindset as Katie as far as wanting to make an inconspicuous entrance to Mary Louise's gathering. Yet, that was hardly possible to do when their innkeeper friend spotted them. As was her custom, she greeted them wholeheartedly and not too quietly.

"You two made it!" Mary Louise clapped her hands. Striding to their sides, she linked one of her arms through each of theirs, introducing them. "Everyone, Katie and Nathan are here. Now we can get the last two celery plants into the ground. They're our final planting couple."

A few people clapped. Others whom he was familiar with, waved. One *Englischer* gave a thumbs-up. All in all, the crowd seemed to be having a good time and were kind in welcoming them. Yet hearing that last word Mary Louise had uttered, he was afraid Katie would be flustered by it. A quick glance at her told him he'd guessed right. While she projected the same congenial smile she always did when hailing customers at the market, her blue eyes weren't as sublime as usual. They were as round as a rabbit caught in a headlight as his *mamm* used to say—even though he'd correct her and say deer.

"Here you go, Katie." Annie stepped up, passing along the hand trowel she'd just used. Andrew handed him a trowel as well before the young pair walked away together.

Watching Katie's hand tighten around the tool's handle, he felt badly for her. Even without knowing anything about the life she'd shared with her husband, he had to imagine their time together had been too short. She'd been uncomfortable enough just seeing all the couples and would-be couples when they first arrived. Possibly they were reminders of what she used to have. But now having to participate in this event had to make her unease even worse. He completely sympathized. "It's just a celery plant," he murmured, trying to reassure her as they walked over to the garden area.

Two pots containing the grown seedlings were set atop the remaining two spots in the garden. As they lowered themselves onto the green kneeling pads in front of those spots, he noticed Katie's creamy cheeks turned crimson. Was she feeling everyone's eyes on them? Or something other than that? He wasn't sure. Still, he felt the urge to comfort her. "Again, it's just a vegetable plant, Katie."

They simultaneously dug their trowels into the dirt. Then placing the plants into their new homes, they patted the soil neatly and solidly around them.

"That wasn't so hard, was it?" He deliberately kept his voice soft as he looked at her. Being so close, the sweet scent of her vanilla soap was even stronger.

"*Nee,* not so hard," she whispered back. Even so, she

swiped her hand across her forehead like a runner who'd just finished a race in the heat of July. As she did, her fingers left a trail of dirt there.

Without a moment's thought, he reached out. Ever so gently, he rubbed her skin to remove the smudge. As soon as he did, he realized it was a mistake. She drew back, looking shocked.

"You could've just told me I had dirt on my face," she whispered.

Yes, he could have. But somehow, he hadn't thought of that. Or had he not wanted to? Even he questioned his thought process—but not for too long. As they stood up, the group began to clap as if they'd just completed a perfect performance on stage.

"That wraps up the planting, you all," Mary Louise proclaimed. "Time to eat."

"Celery casserole?" Nathan recognized an old friend speak up.

"Of course." Mary Louise laughed. "Also, there are sandwiches and other treats too, all from Miller's Market." She glanced at him and Katie. He was thankful she hadn't mentioned those treats had been donated since he didn't want the extra attention. And for sure he knew Katie didn't.

Even so, his being there with Katie did bring Caleb and Judith Peachey striding up to them.

"Nathan, good to see you," Caleb said.

"And congratulations to you and Judith," Nathan replied. The pair hadn't been married too long. That was evident from Caleb's short and still somewhat sparse beard.

"Have you found a reason to keep you here in Blossom Grove now?" Caleb glanced back and forth between him and Katie.

Before he could answer, Katie spoke up. *"Nee, nee.*

We're only friends and coworkers." She smiled. "Why, we can barely make it through a day at work without arguing."

"I'd say it's different with us married folk," Judith spoke up. "But I know *Gott* wouldn't like me to be lying."

Caleb's wife giggled and they all joined in. After a few more minutes of conversation, Katie politely excused herself to go help Mary Louise serve the food. Judith followed behind her. But later while he chatted with other guests, he noticed Judith rejoin Caleb. Whereas, Katie was still keeping her distance. Taking on more hostess duties, she kept busy refilling drinks and removing dirty plates from the folding tables.

After everyone had eaten, and a few couples were lingering, enjoying Mary Louise's hospitality and each other's company, he drifted into the kitchen. He was sure that's where he'd find her. And he was right. From what he could tell, she'd already washed and dried silverware and glasses. It appeared she was just finishing up, drying clean plates.

"May I help you?" he asked coming up behind her.

The way she jumped at the sound of his voice made him think she'd been deeply lost in thought.

"I, uh, I'm almost finished," she answered.

"I can see that." Even though she hadn't accepted his offer, he picked up a dishcloth.

"Be careful of your wrist," she warned.

"Yes, *mamm*." he teased, getting a smile from her.

"I'm too serious sometimes, aren't I?"

"Sometimes?" he jested.

She chuckled in response. Oddly, the sound of her laughter caused a warm feeling to flow over him, surprising him. It was still there slightly as they finished up the dishes in silence.

"I'm kind of thirsty after all that work." Katie turned from putting away the last of the plates. "How about you?"

Even though he'd been with her all day, the idea of spending a little more time together sounded pleasurable. "You rest. I'll get it."

After grabbing freshly washed glasses from the cupboard and then lemon-lime drinks from the refrigerator, he joined Katie where she was seated at the small kitchen table. Laughter and murmurings from guests could still be heard from the other rooms. But he was sure Katie was more comfortable right where she was, away from anyone's questioning eyes. Also, she was at an angle where she could see Annie, Andrew and Rachel playing a board game at a table on the back porch.

"Mary Louise has such a knack for making times and people feel special, doesn't she?" She glanced from the teens to look at him. "Has she had this inn for a long time?"

"From what I know, she and Thomas inherited it from someone in his family."

"*Gott* sure knew what He was doing when He made it theirs."

"It seems He did," he agreed.

"Nathan."

"Katie."

They addressed each other at the same time. He held out the palm of his hand to lead her to speak. "Ladies first."

"*Danke.*" She nodded. Then hesitated, rubbing her thumb up and down the edge of her glass. "Nathan... I was just going to say, please don't feel sorry for me or like you have to be nicer to me because I was adopted. People do that sometimes, and it's silly. I may have been abandoned by my birth parents, but Annie and I had parents who truly loved us. Honestly, I don't even know why I blurted that out and shared that with you." She shook her head.

In the past hours, he'd thought about what she'd revealed to him. More than that, he'd marveled at her. Compared to the situation he'd been born into, she'd had it tough. Abandoned by birth parents. Widowed. Providing for a sister. And yet, she seemed resolved to take it all on, which was what he was going to compliment her on. Since she'd just asked him not to make a big deal of it all, however, he didn't. Rather, he spoke lightly.

"Ah, you know, you probably mentioned it because you're getting used to sharing with me. I mean, look at us. Just in the past week, we've shared a lot together. There's been a broken freezer. And—"

"Hungry raccoons."

"A new store sign—which was a *gut* thing."

"A sucker in a little girl's hair, which was a messy thing."

"And planting celery together."

"And that was kind of a strange thing."

Katie laughed at her own remark, and he was happy to laugh along too. Then settling even more comfortably into their wooden chairs, they took their time sipping their drinks. After a few minutes of gazing at anything but each other, she spoke up.

"Often, my *mamm* and I—well, and Annie too, when she got older—had a habit of sitting and talking once we were done with the dishes. Whether we had cold drinks or hot ones, we'd laugh about how we were messing up the kitchen all over again."

He lifted his half-empty glass. "Well, I can't take the place of your *schweschder* or *mamm*, but I am *gut* at dirtying more dishes."

"Oh, now. You're *gut* at more than that. Sometimes." She smiled.

"You just had to go and add that, didn't you?"

"I don't want you getting a big head."

"Trust me, that's not possible."

He didn't mean for his tone to turn so serious. The kind person that she was, she hugged him with her eyes.

"I bet you're *verra gut* at building houses. How did you end up doing that and in Middlefield anyway?"

"Are you trying to get me to share some more?"

She laughed. "Only if you want to."

Somehow with his new companion, he really did. "For one thing, I feel like *Gott* put it in me to build things."

"I can see that." She nodded. "You try to do the same with the market too."

"Yeah, well..." He shrugged off her compliment, even though coming from her, the good feeling lingered. "As far as Middlefield, I met Daniel Shetler, who's the son of the homebuilder I now work for, when we were on a rescue mission together. And..." He wasn't ready to disclose what had happened between him and the girl from the pizza parlor a couple of nights before. Or to say how building houses has been far easier for him than building a relationship and ultimately a home with someone. But there were some other truths too that had led him to stay in a town a hundred miles away. Those seemed easier to impart.

"I'm the oldest of my siblings," he continued. "And yet, Betsy and Moses seemed to have done a lot more than me. They've married. They have families now. And they've moved away and made lives for themselves. Since I didn't have anything here in Blossom Grove, I felt like it was time for me to leave and make a life for myself too."

"And do you have that in Middlefield?"

He shifted in his chair. "Time will tell, I suppose," he said vaguely but honestly.

"I know what you mean." She sighed. "That's why I plan to do all I can each day to make a home for Annie and me here."

She sounded so strong and determined he didn't doubt she would. Just the same, it was funny how she was trying to make a life in Blossom Grove. And how he'd been trying to avoid it. What a pair they were!

"And, one last question…" She paused, looking him in the eyes.

"Jah?"

"My sweet tooth is calling me. Have you had dessert? There's one last slice of Annie's apple pie left."

"Are you trying to torture me or offering to share?"

"Hmm." She tapped her lips. "Since we've been so good at sharing, I'll do that. But you have to promise me one thing."

He couldn't imagine what she was going to say. Even so, he complied. "Sure, what?"

"Would you consider letting Annie sell some of her baked products in the store?" she asked.

"Oh, I get it. So she'll have more time in the kitchen and less time to spend with her possible new beau?" He raised a brow.

"Did I say that?"

"Not in so many words." He smiled.

"Please don't think I don't want her to spend time being with friends. I do. Maybe Rachel will even help her bake."

"I understand. She can even sell her baked goods at our table at the school fundraiser coming up soon. It's a huge event."

"Really? You'd let her do that?"

"Sure. As long as you promise me something too."

"What's that?"

"I get the bigger piece of the slice."

Laughter bubbled up out of her. Recognizing he'd been able to bring her even the slightest bit of joy, the same warm feeling washed over him again. The short dinner at Bruno's had been nice, but something about this time together was different. Getting more familiar with her felt surprisingly good. For him, at least. Making him realize that it'd been a very long while since he'd enjoyed the company of a girl so much. A girl with such a sound heart and a wholesome glow. Not to mention the bluest eyes he'd ever seen, now that he thought about it.

It was just too bad their time together wasn't meant to last.

Chapter Eight

It was almost a contradiction of sorts, and Katie knew it as she sat across the market's office desk, listening to Nathan. Because as much as she had dreaded Mary Louise's couples planting party a few days earlier, ever since then she'd been finding it more comfortable to be around him. It was easier to talk to him. And she hadn't shied away from laughing with him. Even having him at the reins taking her and Annie and Mary Louise to Sunday worship had brought on a feeling of contentment. Along with all that, there was something that felt oddly safe about the man.

Yet until just now, as he asked Lucy Metzger another interview question, she hadn't been able to figure out where this new ease with him was coming from. And then it hit her. How could she have been bewildered by something so obvious? She could take pleasure in a friendly relationship with Nathan because of one undeniable fact. In two and half weeks, he'd be gone. He'd be a hundred miles away and out of her life for good. It was as uncomplicated as that. Why else had they been conducting numerous interviews in the past days?

Relieved that she'd solved the mystery of her less restrained feelings for him, she let go of a sigh. Then just as quickly, reality hit. A twinge of panic trickled through her stomach. So far, finding a replacement for Nathan hadn't been quite as simple as her new insight—not at all. This week alone, they hadn't agreed on even one person they'd interviewed for the position.

Yet unfortunately for Lucy, Katie was sure she and Nathan would finally be of the same mind this time around. With a toddler clinging to Lucy's skirt and three more *kinner* at home, the pregnant woman was upfront about stating that her available work hours would be very limited. Given that, there was no way she could possibly be a prime candidate for such an all-encompassing job. It wasn't going to be easy, however, to say no to the sweet young *mamm,* given her circumstances. Katie assumed that was exactly why Nathan asked Lucy to excuse them both for a minute. Shuffling from the office, they took their routine spot at the deli counter, outside of Lucy's hearing.

"I know what you're thinking, Nathan," Katie told him, regret welling up inside her once again. Being the interviewer instead of the interviewee and having to say no to people was far more difficult than she would've ever thought.

"You do?" Quirking his brow, he looked surprised, which confused her.

"Well, I think so," she said hesitantly. "I mean, I have a *gut* feeling about Lucy. And her family has had it tough with her husband just getting back to work after his accident. So, my heart goes out to her. I hope they've gotten some aid from the community fund."

"I would be certain that they have. But, Katie, speaking of help, I believe she can help us too."

"Oh, Nathan. Are you serious?" Her shoulders slumped. "I'm sorry, and this isn't easy for me to say, but she doesn't seem to be the right person for the job. She said herself she needs work for only a few hours a week, and we need someone who can devote more time to the store. *Ach*, it's hard. I feel so sorry for her."

"Well..." Nathan drawled out the word. "What would you think if we give her a different kind of job to do like we did with Abram?"

She squinted into his questioning blue eyes, trying to conjure up what that meant. Recently, Abram had replaced some loose shingles. He'd repaired shelving. He'd also hung a new blackboard on the wall behind the cash register. But as far as Lucy doing those kinds of tasks? Katie couldn't imagine it. Lucy had already mentioned that she wasn't handy with a hammer but that she was very good with anything having to do with food. That's why she hoped for a job at the market.

"Do you mean like having her wash fruit?" That was about all Katie could come up with.

Nathan chuckled somewhat at that. "*Nee*. I'm thinking what if we pay Lucy to take the market's donations to the food pantry every other week?"

"You know, when you mentioned the food pantry while we were talking at Bruno's, I meant to tell you that I don't have anything about that written down in my notebook." She bit her lip. "When I was working with Sylvia, she may have forgotten with everything else that was going on then."

"That's makes sense." Nathan nodded. "Well, like I told you, it's something *Aenti* Lovina and *Onkel* Jacob used to always do, and I'd like to keep that tradition alive. If Lucy takes care of it, that would be one less job for you and whoever we hire to work with you. And she can make a little money while also dropping in on a place where she can get free food."

It didn't seem like a bad idea. At least it would be something they could offer Lucy. Still, she wavered. "Is there enough money to hire her along with paying Abram and whoever will be my new coworker?"

"That's not for you to worry about," he replied decisively.

Not worry? Oh, if he only knew how serious and stressful the issue of money was for her. Not that she would ever say so.

"How did you even come up with this idea anyway?" she asked, curious. "Do you know Lucy's family?"

"*Nee*, but I know you."

"I'm not sure what you mean."

"Well, you'll be here working and every time you see Lucy and her *kinner* come into the market, you're going to feel badly. You're going to wish you'd done something to help. And…" He paused, gazing into her eyes. "Very recently—oh, I'd say around the time Abram started here—someone taught me how to give everyone and every situation a second look."

It wasn't as if he'd never smiled at her with his lips or even with his eyes once in a while. Yet standing so close to him, hearing how well he knew her, her heart responded with a surprising flutter. Caught off guard, she crossed her arms over her chest as if that could squash the sensation.

"But, Katie, it's up to you," Nathan continued. "You have to be *oll recht* with this decision. After all, soon you'll be Miller's store manager."

Up to her? Store manager? That came unexpectedly from her "overseer."

She straightened and cleared her throat, hoping to sound as professional as the title. "Nathan, I know business has picked up, and the market is doing far better. But again, I still believe it's all a question of money."

"And again…" He grinned. "I'll take care of it. Will you

trust me?" A wavy lock of his light brown hair fell to his forehead. Pushing it back into place with his fingers, he fully beseeched her with his gaze.

Hearing those words, seeing that look, her heart clutched in her chest as memories flooded her. *But this isn't that same man,* she kept telling herself, glancing at Nathan. *You're in a new place now.* She tried to reassure herself, looking around the market.

"Katie?"

Nathan's voice drew her out of the pit of her angst.

"Let's go tell Lucy and see what she thinks of your idea," she replied. "Like you said, hopefully it will help all of us."

His eyes lit up once more at her response, and he smiled. This time, however, she made sure to look away.

Katie noted that it was near closing time when Nathan turned to her, asking if she'd be okay working by herself for a while.

"I need to step out for a bit," he said, not offering to say more.

She was curious about where he was headed. Even so, it was none of her business. "I'll be fine," she assured him.

Due to the time of day, store traffic had slowed down in the past hour. She'd been able to attend to end-of-the-day chores like straightening mussed bins and righting items on shelves. And she would've been pleased to continue doing just that. But of course, as soon as Nathan walked out the door, over a handful of customers streamed in. Instead of taking their time wandering around the market, they quickly grabbed the items they needed. Before she knew it, she was behind the cash register, facing a long checkout line.

Thankfully, the first two customers in line only had a

handful of items, which she rang up quickly. But that wasn't so with the third person, one of the Yoder twins. Iva had a full cart, and she didn't appear one bit moved to let the others behind her go ahead of her. Either that or she was truly oblivious to the fact that those customers only had single items in their hands.

About halfway through ringing up Iva's groceries, Katie felt guilty she wasn't going any faster. Lifting her head, she apologized to them all. "Sorry, for the delay, everyone. I appreciate your patience."

"Take your time, dear *maedel*." Effie Hess stepped out from the last spot in line, behind all the others to offer her support. Katie would've recognized the elderly woman's kind voice even without seeing her petite chubby frame. "You're doing just fine," Effie added.

Effie's encouragement brought on a wave of comfort. Smiling, Katie looked up over the heads of the customers in line, wanting to tell Effie thanks. Then she saw a man, an *Englischer* dressed in dress pants and a sport coat and froze. Apparently, he'd come in without her noticing, and he hadn't gone far. He stood twirling the rack of garden seed packets while glancing around the market and up toward the checkout counter. Watching him and seeing that he had no interest in any item in the store, her heart lurched. Was he another person trying to get money out of her? Had he found her in this town?

Dear Gott, please help me. Please. I've already lost all I ever had!

"You rang up the tangerines twice," Iva told her, breaking into her frenzy of thoughts.

"Oh, I'm… I'm so sorry. Let me correct that."

Her hands trembled uncontrollably as she tapped the cash register screen. Her mind scrambled as she packed

Iva's groceries. Finally, daring to glance up again, she saw that the man had disappeared. But not for one second did she feel any relief. Her insides continued to shake frantically. She had to wonder. Was he only outside waiting?

"Are you sure your *oll recht*, Katie?"

Nathan had come to appreciate the soft pure look of her ivory complexion. But ever since he'd returned from the bank and they'd shut down the market, a paleness had enveloped her cheeks like he'd never seen. When he had glanced at her shaky hands, she'd noticed and turned from his caring gaze, tucking them in her apron pockets. That's where her hands still were as he worked to keep up with her quick stride down the sidewalk.

"I'm fine. Just fine," she muttered, turning to look behind them for the tenth time.

"Katie, you don't seem fine. Is there anything I can do for you?"

She turned around and gasped. He turned as well, only to see a group of teenagers and a few adults behind them who were barely visible.

"*Jah,* you can hurry," she said. "We need to hurry." She grabbed his hand.

"To where?" he asked.

"To the drugstore before they close. I need to buy a greeting card."

He didn't understand what was going on with her, but he let himself be pulled along without asking a question. Until they were in the store and standing by the racks of cards, and she wasn't even looking in the direction of them.

"Katie," he said softly, wanting to pull her close to him to calm her. But he stopped himself, placing his hands on her shoulders. "Please, tell me. How can I help? What's scaring you?"

She bit her lip, searching his gaze, which he hoped she could find refuge in. "There was a man at the market. An *Englischer*. He was acting strangely."

"Strangely how? Like he was going to steal something?"

"Nee. No, not that."

"What then?" He wanted to know for her sake.

"I… I…" She wrung her hands, then looked away from him. "I can't explain. But then I saw him again, following us."

She couldn't explain? Or didn't want to? From the way she was acting and suddenly avoiding eye contact, he wasn't quite sure.

But whatever the case, it didn't matter. Instantly, protective feelings surged in him. If anyone dared harm her, he didn't know what he'd do. "This man, did he hurt you? Did he say something? Did he—"

She interrupted him with another gasp. "He's here. Nathan, he's coming toward us."

He could almost hear her heart beating as she stiffly nodded at whoever was coming up behind him. His hands instantly turned into fists as he angled around. Just as quickly, his grip relaxed.

"Mr. Zimmerman," he exclaimed.

"James to you." Coming right up to him, the *Englischer* clapped him on the shoulder. "I can't believe I'm getting to see you, Nathan. I was passing through Blossom Grove on my way home from a business trip and stopped in at the market. When I didn't see you there, I figured I was out of luck. Just so happened I thought I'd come in here for a pack of gum while I'm waiting for my carryout order."

He turned from him to Katie. "You've got yourself quite a catch here, young lady," he said to her.

To which he was just as taken aback as Katie was.

"Oh, *nee*, Nathan and I, we're just friends." She shook her head. But he noticed not at all as forcefully as she had the weekend before. Also, a rosy color began to dot her cheeks. From James's implication? Or because she suddenly appeared to be calming down? "So, you two know each other?" She glanced between them.

James readily answered. "We've hardly ever been in contact with one another over the years. But I know all I need to know about this guy." James gave him a friendly fist bump in his stomach before addressing Katie again. "I live with my family about thirty miles from here, and one summer I came to Lake Lorelei to do some fishing with my son. Again, this was years ago. As it turned out, my wallet fell out of my pocket on the bank of the lake. I didn't realize it until I got back home. To tell you the truth, I figured I'd never see it again or the hundreds of dollars inside it. But then this guy…"

James paused to nudge him in the chest with his elbow. Nathan's hand automatically flew to the spot. For sure, he'd forgotten what a manly man James was.

"He mailed the wallet to me," James continued. "So, I came back to town to give him a reward. He was in his late teens working at the market then. He refused to take the money. Can you believe it?"

Nathan noticed Katie didn't reply if she did believe that of him or not. Although in a way, he couldn't feel too badly. She barely had a chance to answer since James kept chattering.

"Nathan, since I didn't see you at the market, what are you up to these days?"

"Oh, I am at the market helping out temporarily. Just till my wrist heals." He held up his sprinted hand. "I must've just stepped out when you came in."

"So, you're not long for the market then?"

"*Nee*. I've been working for an Amish homebuilder in Middlefield now. I'll be returning there in a couple of weeks." Even as he said that out loud, it didn't sound as rousing as it used to. Though for the life of him, he didn't know why.

"Well, I'm sure everyone feels fortunate to have you back in town for a short while, at least," James replied.

Nathan chuckled. "We'll see about that," he said, giving Katie a quick glance. Her greenish blue eyes flickered at him with good humor, causing him to wonder. Was that it? Was *she* the reason Middlefield sounded like more than a hundred miles away? He was so startled by the notion that he barely heard all James was saying.

"...and that being said... I ordered Amish chicken dinners to take home to the family. Something they all requested." James peeked at his watch. "I'm sure they're ready for pick up now. But I'm really glad I got to run into you. Both of you."

"It was *wunderbaar* to see you too, Mr.—James. You have safe travels."

"You know where to find me if you ever need me," James offered.

"*Danke*. That means a lot." This time Nathan took his turn clasping James on the shoulder before the *Englischer* turned to go.

Moments after James left them, Katie started to head toward the door as well. Still standing by the card rack, he was puzzled.

"Katie, I thought you wanted to look for a card," he called after her.

"Oh, I can do that later." She waved a hand at him.

He shrugged and caught up with her. As they sauntered down the sidewalk toward the inn, she kept giving him curious looks.

"What?" he finally asked her. "I know there's something you want to say."

Her footsteps stopped, and he could sense a shyness coming over her. Even so, she raised her chin to him. "I'm just wondering, did it ever cross your mind not to give that wallet back and to keep the money?"

He wasn't sure what she wanted to hear. But the earnestness in her expression seemed to be pleading for his honesty. "I'd be lying if I said that it didn't," he replied.

Maybe it wasn't the best answer he could've given, but it was the truth. She stared at him for a moment and then nodded as if satisfied. Everything inside him relaxed with relief. Because he knew he'd also be lying if he didn't care about her approval. Not only that, he'd be fibbing if he wasn't curious about her and wanted to protect her too.

Whatever had frightened her so much, he had no real clue. She'd been vague. Yet, one thing was clear. She hadn't felt comfortable opening up to him, and he wasn't sure why. Even so, he couldn't pretend any longer that everything she was going through—or had gone through—made no difference to him. Because every day, more and more, everything about Katie did matter to him. Too much, in fact.

In a way, that was frightening too.

Chapter Nine

After hearing Nathan's admission, Katie felt unsteady with every step on their way back to the inn. Yet, it wasn't her feet that faltered. It was her emotions. Her feelings kept fluctuating from being astonished by Nathan and somewhat uncomfortable with herself. Because besides her own father, she'd never had a man be so honest with her as Nathan had just been. When she'd asked if he'd considered keeping the lost wallet, he hadn't stuck out his chest, bragging that such verboten thoughts were beneath him. Nor had he acted shocked that she might think he was even capable of such a thing. No, he'd been truthful. Forthright. Even to the extent of making himself appear, well, human.

And while she'd never disagreed with Annie's appraisal that Nathan was a good-looking man, now when she dared to glance at him, there was even more to find attractive about him. His frankness was charming. The humble sincerity in his voice, fetching. All of which suddenly made her feel so much closer to him. Not that that was a good thing. It wasn't good at all. Not when it left her struggling and feeling guilt-ridden too.

True, Nathan would be gone soon. But out of decency, if he'd been so open with her, shouldn't she be the same with him? Maybe confess that she'd been a wee bit—okay, not candid at all—about her initial fear of the *Englisch* man? And how it related to her late husband?

Her heart rate quickened at the thought of disclosing everything about her past with Jonathan Lantz—or even some of it. Where would she start with all his deception and the mockery he'd made of their marriage? Not to mention, how the catastrophic ending of their so-called love story left her nearly penniless. And if she did relay all of it to Nathan, wouldn't that be risky? For sure, he could think she was too gullible, too naive to be responsible for running the market. How could she explain in a positive way that the horrid circumstances she'd experienced had left her more cynical and cautious? And would he believe her as she'd just now believed him?

She glanced at Nathan, seeing him looking straight ahead. He'd been unusually quiet the entire walk. With the head he had on his shoulders, she didn't doubt he suspected she was hiding something from the way she'd carried on. Once more, her conscience niggled at her. She didn't want to lie to him, knowing firsthand how much lies ruined everything, most importantly, trust. Then again, she warred with herself. Being honest could jeopardize her and Annie's future all over again, ain't so? Though a nauseous feeling filled her gut, she knew what she had to do. If Nathan did ask questions once they settled inside the hushed retreat of the inn, she'd have to be upfront and truthful.

Yet, the closer they got to the inn, there didn't appear to be anything quiet about the place.

"Look at all the buggies and bikes." Nathan pointed to the front and side streets, uttering her thoughts. "Wonder what Mary Louise is up to?"

"You know what? I bet ladies are here finishing up quilts

to auction off at the school fundraiser. She'd mentioned they still had work to do."

Sure enough, a cacophony of women's voices and giggles filled the inn as they ventured inside. The atmosphere was far from relaxing. Every seat in the usually cozy sitting room was filled with a woman bent over her work, chattering. The dining room was the same way with a half dozen chairs pushed away from the table, along with a few extras placed against the walls.

"I have a feeling it's not going to be *verra* quiet around here this evening," Nathan said.

Realizing there was probably little chance of a serious talk amidst so much chaos, she let out sigh of relief. Even so, that feeling of consolation evaporated quickly when Annie walked out of the kitchen. Because there he was again—Andrew. Right at her sister's side, he stood with cupcake containers in his hands.

"Hello?" Katie didn't mean for her greeting to come out as a question. But she couldn't help it since the pair looked like they were off to somewhere. Besides that, she had to ask the same thing that seemed to be routine lately. "Where's Rachel?"

"She tripped in the kitchen earlier and hurt her ankle," Annie readily replied. "Her *mamm* came to get her. Andrew heard, and he'd finished his chores, so he came over to help me finish up the cupcakes. Wasn't that nice of him?"

Katie's mouth dropped open, while Nathan gave a little cough in reply. Glancing over at him, she saw his curled-up hand, covering the amused grin on his face. She knew he had to be inwardly gloating. It seemed his initial impression of the Annie-and-Andrew situation might've been right on target. First, this sixteen-year-old boy had been planting celery and now he was icing cupcakes? Was he really that smitten?

She wanted to groan out loud. "And now you think you're going where?" she asked in a way that hadn't given her sister permission yet.

"Well, you know that I've been filling Mary Louise's freezer with baked goods for the fundraiser."

"Jah." Katie nodded. "I do know that."

"And now an *Englischer* neighbor of the Glicks has offered more freezer space at their house. So, Andrew and I are taking these containers of cupcakes there."

"You're walking?" Katie looked between her sister and Andrew.

"It's not too bad of a walk," Andrew answered shyly.

"Also, Mrs. Glick invited me to stay for dinner. She spoke to Mary Louise about it," Annie hurried to add. "Mary Louise didn't think you'd mind since it's so busy around here. You don't care, do you?"

"Well, I..." She hesitated, knowing she had no dinner plans of her own. For some reason, she found herself glancing over at Nathan as if he might have an answer. She knew he'd been looking around the dining room trying to stay removed from the conversation. Or rather, her interrogation. Then suddenly he whipped his head around and angled toward her. Out of nowhere, it seemed his stubbled face had turned ashen.

"How about I hitch up Mary Louise's Rusty to her buggy, and we'll drop the kids off at the Glicks," he suggested. "Then we can go to see my *onkel* at Sylvia's place. Speaking of the fundraiser, I have some questions for him."

Nathan seemed to want to get out of there and quickly. For sure, the women's chitchat was at high decibels. But she didn't believe that's why he'd suddenly appeared so disturbed. Yet at the moment, the reason truly didn't matter to her. With Annie and Andrew in the buggy, she could at least chaperone them all the way to the Glicks' house. And since she'd gotten to know Barbara Glick a bit better from seeing her at worship service, she trusted Barbara would do the same once they arrived.

"I'd love to meet your *onkel* Jacob and visit with Sylvia and Clyde."

"Let's get going then."

Nathan hastened them from the inn and didn't waste any time getting Rusty ready to go. Yet a short time later, after dropping off Annie and Andrew, Katie noticed a distinct change in him. It seemed the farther they got from the town, the more he appeared to relax. Whereas, unfortunately, that wasn't so with her.

Sure, she was around Nathan mostly all day and some evenings. But they were generally working and typically there were other people all around. Now she couldn't remember the last time she'd been alone with a man in a buggy. Her hands were clenched together in her lap. And she needed to stop nervously biting her lip. Somehow, talking seemed to be the answer to making their solitude less notable.

"Thank you for taking Annie and Andrew in the buggy, Nathan."

He looked over at her with a knowing smile. "I could see the worried look in your eyes when Annie said they were going to be walking that distance together."

"Just the idea of them being alone, even in the kitchen, and Annie getting so close to him. Physically and emotionally." She shook her head. "It makes me—"

"*Verrickt*? Crazy? No one would ever know from that pent-up expression of yours." He chuckled, then patted her shoulder consolingly. "Don't be too hard on yourself. You're just trying to protect your sister. But I do have to ask, didn't you ever have a crush at her age?"

"Well, maybe one…" She paused. "Or two…" She wiggled a pair of fingers in the air playfully.

"Or three or four?" He laughed.

"Now you're going overboard." She chuckled. "And how about you back then? Or even now? You seemed like you were in a hurry to leave the inn. Was there some *maedel* there who was always smitten on you?"

She only meant to be fun-loving. When his mouth gaped and his hands tightened on the reins, she wished she hadn't said as much.

"I, uh…" He bit his lower lip. "I saw someone who I haven't seen in a while. We exchanged glances. How did you know?"

"You sort of acted the same way when we were at Bruno's. You were in a rush to get somewhere else. I figured then it was because of a girl too."

"You're mighty perceptive."

Oh, if only she'd been more that way a couple of years ago.

"But how about we leave the past behind us for right now," he suggested. "It's a *wunderbaar* evening. The sun's still out, and as my *mamm* used to say, 'regrets over yesterday and the fear of tomorrow—'"

"'—are twin thieves that rob us of the moment.'" She completed the bit of wisdom. "My *mamm* used to say as much too."

"So then, let's just live in the moment right now." His smile was easygoing as he quirked his brow questioningly. Then as he slowly reached his hand toward her, she suddenly imagined he might be about to caress her cheek. Her pulse raced in response. An unexpected warmth trickled up her neck. But then, instead of feeling the softness of his touch, he tugged playfully on her *kapp* string. "That okay with you?" he asked.

"Ha!" She gasped, relieved. "For sure and certain," she replied. To prove it, she also extended her hand, dipping his hat over his eyebrows.

They laughed at each other as she righted her *kapp*, and he pushed back his straw hat from his forehead.

Without a doubt, it did feel special being in the present. Not only that, realizing Nathan also wasn't keen on divulging what he'd been running from, she could relax more too. As he'd said, they could both leave the past behind for the time being. Enjoy the scenery and each other's company. They could put off till tomorrow what should've been said today.

Nathan was extremely thankful that after exchanging awkward glances and nods with Sarah Fisher back at the inn, he'd had someplace to run off to. Also, he'd had an appreciative woman to accompany him. Even watching Katie's eyes widen as they pulled into his *Aenti* Sylvia and *Onkel* Clyde's expansive property, brought him a snippet of joy. That was along with her appreciative sigh.

"Oh, my," she whispered softly.

While the Mast house itself was a tidy and simple two-bedroom ranch with a porch running the length of it, the landscape surrounding the home wasn't modest in the least. Obviously, from Katie's reaction as she scanned the rolling hills dotted with grazing horses and splashes of wildflowers and copious newly blooming trees, she didn't think so either. She hopped out of the buggy quickly and stood, taking in the view. After hitching Rusty and joining her, he was just as pleased to check out the familiar scenery *Gott* had provided once again.

"It's nice, ain't so?" he asked, crossing his arms over this chest.

"It's like everything you see on these winding roads but all in one place here," she exclaimed. "It's beautiful."

Seeing her awestruck expression, he caught himself thinking the same about her. Instantly, he shook his head to rid himself of that notion. What was with him lately?

It helped when his thoughts were interrupted by the sound of a screen door creaking along with his aunt's voice.

"Nathan? Katie? I saw you through the window. What a *wunderbaar* surprise! Come in, you two."

As they stepped into the house and followed Sylvia to the kitchen, the aroma of roast beef greeted them as much as her smile had. "We just finished supper, but there's plenty left if you haven't eaten. You're welcome to have a seat." She glanced toward the kitchen table, which was nearly cleared off.

"It looks like you about have it all cleaned up, *Aenti.*"

"And we're fine, *danke,*" Katie piped up. "We had a late lunch."

He didn't quite recall them having lunch at all. Knowing Katie was trying to be polite, however, he agreed. "Besides, we can't stay long. We only wanted to stop by and say hello, and to ask *Onkel* Jacob a few questions about the upcoming fundraiser. Are he and Clyde in the sitting room?"

Worry lines immediately creased his aunt's forehead as she tucked her hands into her apron pockets. "Clyde is out in the barn. And, *jah*, my *bruder* is in there." She tilted her head toward the living area. "But I don't know how much you're going to get out of him. He barely talks, just often sits and stares. He's supposed to be walking each day and building up the distance. But I don't know how that's going to happen because he doesn't always do it. And he—"

"Sylvia, I can hear you talking about me." His uncle's gruff bark came from the other room. "I may have had heart trouble, but I am not deaf."

Sylvia winced, rolling her eyes. "All I can say is, may *Gott* be with you," she whispered to him and Katie, shaking her head.

As soon as Nathan laid eyes on his uncle, he could readily see that Sylvia wasn't wrong in what she was saying. It didn't appear much had changed with his uncle since he'd last seen him a couple of weeks earlier. His whitish-gray beard was still unkempt. His nails had grown even longer. He sat huddled in the reclining chair as if it were a throne he was never about to be toppled from.

Seeing the uncle who used to be so jolly and positive in this state, he felt dismay gnaw at him. Even so, he tried to sound upbeat. "*Onkel* Jacob, it's so good to see you. I brought a special person here for you to meet. This is Katie Troyer."

Katie stepped forward as his uncle cocked a brow. "Katie? The girl Sylvia told me about?"

So, his uncle did listen some and knew what was going on after all. "Yes, the same person."

"Hmm." From behind his wire-rimmed glasses, his uncle looked her up and down, leaving an awkward silence.

That is, until Katie, being Katie, took it upon herself to ease the situation the same way she did with customers. "Mr. Miller, I'm so glad to finally meet you. I've been wanting to tell you myself how much I appreciate you letting me work at your wonderful market. I really enjoy it and promise to do my best. And..." She leaned a bit closer.

"Just to let you know, Nathan acts like I'm deaf too. He repeats things to me all the time at work."

Nathan cringed at first, not sure how his uncle would react since he wasn't the jolly person he used to be. But then seeing his uncle crack a slight smile, he eagerly played along. "Katie, really? You're saying I do that? You're saying that about me?"

"See?" Katie turned to his uncle, crooking her shoulder. "There he goes again, repeating himself. As if I didn't hear him the first time."

His uncle full-out laughed at that. Hearing the sound erupt from him was heartening for Nathan. He could tell from Katie's smile that she was touched as well.

"You do that to this sweet *maedel*?" his uncle asked him.

Nathan kept up the guise. "Only because sometimes she doesn't seem to be listening to me."

"Maybe that's a *gut* thing." His uncle chortled.

"Jah." Katie put her hands on her hips. "You should listen to your *onkel*, Nathan. He's a smart man."

An hour later after talking to his uncle a bit about the fundraiser and chuckling about life in general, it was time to go. Nathan helped Katie into the buggy since she was toting a bag of roast beef sandwiches and chips that Sylvia insisted on giving them.

Before he even led Rusty out of the driveway, Katie's enthusiasm about the evening seemed uncontainable. And he had to admit, contagious.

"Oh, Nathan, that was wonderful, don't you think? I mean, I really enjoyed working with Sylvia and Clyde. They were so *gut* to me. And now, meeting your uncle. What a stitch he is! He can be *verra* witty."

"Trust me, it was hard for me to see him so down when I was staying there. I really think you brought out the best in him, Katie." He hoped she could see the gratitude in his eyes. "As we were leaving, Sylvia whispered to me that she hadn't seen him light up like that in a long while."

"I would think his own *kinner* would come cheer him up."

"Actually, he and my *Aenti* Lovina never had children. I always heard there were many miscarriages and then nothing. And, Sylvia and Clyde had two *dochders* and a son, but they never got baptized. The girls became nurses, and Aaron is an agricultural professor."

"Interesting..." Katie paused. "Well, your relatives are so *wunderbaar*, Nathan. You must feel blessed to have them in your life."

"*Jah*, I do."

Yet as Rusty clip-clopped over the winding road, he realized it wasn't only the relatives he'd just left behind that he felt blessed by. He also felt fortunate to have Katie sitting in the buggy next to him. Stealing a glimpse at her, she looked as pleased as punch as she clutched the bag in her lap and smiled at the road before them. Just the sight of her appearing so pleased gladdened him. And made him want to do something nice for her too.

"After we pick up Annie, want to stop at Daisy's Dairy Whip?"

"Oh, I'd love that, Nathan." Her voice had an excited trill. "I know Annie would too. *Danke* for thinking of it."

Her smile was even broader as they made their way down the road. And, at first, he didn't realize that his was too. Who would have ever guessed that this girl who was new to Blossom Grove would make him feel like everything in town was new to him too?

Hours later when a knock came on his bedroom door, Nathan's first thought was it might be Katie. Instead, it was

Mary Louise bearing an armful of clean towels. He opened the door wider, taking them from her hands.

"You're doing laundry this late in the evening? And after the busy day and all the company you had? Really, Mary Louise, you need to stop and get some rest."

"Oh, I'll be fine. I'm not as old as I'm looking today." She chuckled.

"Old? You look fresh as a daisy. No one can begin to keep up with you."

"Honestly, Nathan…" She tilted her head. "The towels were just an excuse."

"An excuse for what?" he asked, puzzled.

"A reason for me to knock on your door and tell you that I'm sorry. I should've warned you about Sarah being here. Actually, I didn't know at first that she was coming. It was very last minute."

"Don't feel badly, Mary Louise. We were bound to run into each other. In fact, I'd seen her at Bruno's. She just didn't see me."

"Well, I saw you two exchange glances and then noticed how uncomfortable you looked when you rushed out."

"It was all *gut*. It turned out to be a *verra gut* evening all around." Far more enjoyable than he'd first envisioned it being.

"Katie said the same," Mary Louise told him.

"She did?" Instantly, he couldn't stop the corner of his mouth from curving into a smile. "Well, *gut*." There was that word again.

Mary Louise offered a caring grin. "You know, Nathan, as far as you and Sarah, the two of you didn't work out because you weren't supposed to."

"That's not the way the rest of the town saw it. Especially her *daed* who was the deacon then. And I bet there are still some folks who aren't quick to forget how it all played out. In a way, I don't blame them. I didn't handle things well with her."

"Well, I know what I saw between you two." Mary Louise's forehead creased. "Er, I mean what I didn't see. Besides, you have no reason to feel badly. Everything has worked out wonderfully for Sarah and Levi."

"I would think so," he replied. Even back when they were all younger, his best friend and his girl at the time had always enjoyed one another's company.

"And I know so," Mary Louise retorted. "I also know things are going to work out for you too. *Gott* has a plan for you. And you know how I know these things."

He chuckled. "Oh, I do. But enough about me, Mary Louise. You need to get some rest."

She yawned in reply "*Jah,* it has been a day, hasn't it?"

"Yes, it has," he agreed.

"You should relax too."

After saying good-night to Mary Louise, he took her advice. He kicked off his shoes, picked up a book and stretched out on top of his bed. Yet knowing the woman he'd spent such an eventful day with was upstairs above his head, he couldn't stop thinking of her. Or wondering... how it was going to feel when she wasn't simply a staircase away.

Chapter Ten

"**W**ant to double-check me?"

Katie had been busy, packing up small bags of chips and pretzels to sell at the town's semiannual school fundraiser, when Nathan asked the question. She knew he was only being polite as he finished filling up the large plastic container setting on the market's checkout counter.

Yet since he'd just teased her about continually blowing wisps of fallen hair from her forehead during her packing frenzy, she teased right back. "Check you? Or that container?" she jested.

"Preferably the container since I haven't shaved for a couple of days." He scratched at his stubbled chin.

Smiling, she shuffled over to him and peeked inside the bin. She made a mental note—for the time being at least—of the number of plastic silverware boxes and packets of paper plates and napkins he'd packed. "It looks like everything we'll need for serving hot dogs, bratwursts and Mary Louise's potato salad."

And everything that had been on her list of smaller necessary items. Since the days leading up to the fundraiser had been full of prep work, she'd constantly been making entries in her notebook. She'd needed to record as many reminders as she could for future reference. The fall event would be much the same as the spring moneymaker for the Amish school and community medical fund. But it would be far different too. She'd be organizing it all on her own without Nathan as her guide. Or by her side. Like he was just now.

"I think so too," he agreed. "I just wanted you to see what I packed so that if it turns out to be too much or too little, you'll have a better idea what's needed in the fall," he told her. "Even though September is months from now."

Months from now didn't sound long enough as the thought of ultimately being in charge nearly took her breath away. It also tugged at her heart. Even though she and Nathan bickered at times and didn't always see eye to eye, for sure and certain she'd miss having him around. They'd established a relationship after all.

A working relationship. A friendly friendship. Did she need to jot down that reminder in her notebook too?

"I appreciate it, Nathan," she told him. "And to let you know, the bags of chips, pretzels and buns are all packed up. Also, Annie's busy getting the rest of her baked goods from the refrigerated compartments." She pointed over her shoulder down the aisle. "Can you think of anything else?"

She sure couldn't. Nathan had already stored hot dogs, bratwurst, ketchup, relish and mustard in ice-filled coolers. Mary Louise said she'd deliver her potato salad to their table at the fairgrounds. Also, Abram and Andrew promised to haul a pair of large charcoal grills to their space there.

"I just need to gather up cartons of canned drinks," he answered. "With my *gut* hand," he added after she shot him a cautious look. "While I'm doing that, can you do me a favor?"

"Sure, what?"

"Do you mind writing on the sidewalk board that we're closed for the fundraiser today?"

Katie was fairly certain most of the community would assume Miller's Market wouldn't be open. Especially since most other businesses were closed as well. Not only that, she'd been told that nearly everyone in Blossom Grove would be at the event, including hundreds of *Englischers* and Amish from out of town. But she couldn't fault Nathan for being overly communicative. That was rare for a man, including him at times, she thought, smiling to herself.

"I don't mind at all."

"And if it's not too hard, can you add something artsy like you do? Maybe draw a book or a pen or something?"

"A book or a pen?" She chuckled. "How about I sketch a squirrel wearing glasses with an open book in its hands?"

"I was hoping you'd add your special touch."

His grin was so big it still tickled her as she gathered colored chalk and a cloth and headed outside. If he only knew how much she enjoyed the chance to do something so whimsical, he wouldn't be shy about asking.

After twenty or so minutes of drawing and amusing herself, she was almost sad to finish. Tucking the chalk and cloth in her apron pockets, she moved the board closer to the door. As she did, a twinge of pain shot through her finger.

The discomfort must've registered on her face. Nathan questioned her the moment she walked back into the store.

"Katie, what's wrong?"

"Oh, nothing." She waved her hand. "Just a little splinter."

"May I see?"

Without waiting for her answer, he stepped closer. He held out his helping hand. She stared at his outstretched palm, and hesitated. Did she dare?

Finally deciding not to make a fuss, she gave in to the man she knew to be a rescuer of sorts. She placed her hand upright into his.

"Ah, at least it's easy to see," he said. "This sliver of sharp wood is anything but little." With his head bent over her hand, he observed the fragment while she studied the twists and turns of his wavy hair. It seemed a far better way to occupy her mind instead of overthinking the warmth of his touch and concern. Within seconds, he pulled the splinter from its place. He held it up for her to see before brushing it away on his pants leg.

She'd been so engaged in watching him she hadn't realized he was still holding onto her hand—until he grasped it fully and lightly.

"Katie, I promise I'll get Abram to smooth out the wooden edges of the sidewalk board. You don't need to get any more splinters. Not that you can't handle it if you do. But I'd still feel badly since I won't be here for you."

He squeezed her hand ever so gently. Her gaze met his as he looked into her eyes. Suddenly, his leaving felt more real than it ever had before. In less than two weeks, he really would be departing, just as planned. She'd have the chance to become the self-reliant person she'd promised herself to be. He'd be getting on with his life a hundred miles away.

Wasn't that the way it was supposed to be?

All at once, their first day on the job together flashed through her mind. By the end of their shift then, she'd been quick to count the days till she could say good riddance. Now, with her hand in his, she found herself wishing for more days that he'd be staying. Realizing that, her breath hitched. She quickly pulled away from his grasp.

"We better get back to work," she said. "The fundraiser starts in a couple of hours."

"*Jah.* Back to work." He nodded. But his blue eyes stayed poised on hers, causing her cheeks to burn. Aiming to put a stop to that, she wiggled her fingers in the air, breaking their visual connection.

"*Danke* for your help with the splinter, Nathan. I'm going to go see if Annie needs a hand with anything." *Hand*! Why did she have to bring up that word again?

"And it looks like Clyde just pulled up with his wagon." He glanced out the window. "He and I can get started loading some of the coolers."

"Be careful of his back and your hand." Oh, she'd said it again. She cringed. "I mean, your wrist."

Meanwhile, Nathan chuckled. "That's one thing I won't miss. Your constant harping and worrying."

"Oh, *jah,* you'll miss me. Or I mean, you'll miss my harping," she said over her shoulder, scurrying away.

With her cheeks still flushed, she made her way back to the refrigerated compartments. It appeared Annie had just finished retrieving her baked goods. They were neatly stacked in boxes along with her sweets from the inn. Andrew and Rachel had promised to bring the remaining cupcakes from their neighbor's freezer to the fairgrounds.

The moment her sister saw her, Annie crossed her arms over her chest. "What was that all about?"

"What was what all about?" Katie pretended not to understand.

"That thing between you and Nathan. I saw it all, Katie."

"There is no thing—nothing—between us." She shrugged, indifferently.

"Holding hands is nothing?" Her sister arched a brow.

"We weren't holding hands. I had a splinter."

"A splinter, huh? That you couldn't get out yourself?" Her sister's eyes twinkled. "How convenient." She snickered. "And here, you two were so *verra* close. But then, you're always telling me to keep my distance from *buwes*."

"Which you haven't done with Andrew Glick, that's for sure and certain."

"He's just a friend, Katie."

"Uh-huh. Sure." Now it was her turn to quirk her brow.

"Well, maybe more." Annie gave a hopeful grin that immediately turned to a wary frown. "We'll see. Who knows what will happen with his *Rumpsringa* starting soon?"

"You know I only say to be careful of *buwes* because I don't want you to get hurt. Don't you, Annie?"

"And what about you, Katie?"

"Me? I don't know what you mean."

Annie cracked a smile. "Oh, *jah*, you do, *schweschder*. You and Nathan have been spending a lot of time together. I haven't heard you laugh so much since—well, since I don't know when."

"Pffff." She swiped a dismissive hand in the air. "That's so different, Annie."

"It is?" Her sister's eyes narrowed and dimmed somewhat, appearing disappointed. No doubt about it, Annie was fond of Nathan and had been from the very start. Whereas with Jonathan, she'd mainly kept her distance—when and if he was ever around. Apparently, her younger sister's instincts had been far better than her own. If only she'd been wise enough not to be taken in by him, and the man he pretended to be. They wouldn't have lost everything they ever owned. That included her ability to trust her heart again.

"Well, sure. Nathan's going to be leaving soon. Simple as that," she said firmly. "We'll part on friendly terms. Because that's what we are—friends." That was it. Case closed. And the only reason she'd been feeling so safe to be around him.

"And you're okay with that?" Annie asked, once again looking dismayed.

Oh, if only her sister knew half of what had taken place with Jonathan. Then maybe she'd understand. She'd done her best to shield Annie from as much as she could. And for her sister's sake, she wasn't willing to take any chances on a relationship again.

"Of course, I am," she replied confidently. Yet, the lingering feel of her hand in his begged to differ. Trying to squelch the sensation, she immediately did what she did best. Busying herself, she grabbed onto the box of her sister's baked goods. "Let's get this loaded into Clyde's wagon," she said. "It's almost time to go."

For Nathan too, an inner voice taunted her. As if she didn't know.

No one had asked Nathan if he was anxious about heading up Miller Market's part in the fundraiser event. If they had, he probably would've shrugged his shoulders and not given much of an answer anyway. But if truth be known, he'd had his concerns. Why wouldn't he? The school fundraisers he'd been involved in with his aunt and uncle in his younger years had seemed seamless. Easygoing. Right on target. Delightful. And a great moneymaker for the school. He didn't want to ruin that record.

Now standing behind one of Miller's three folding tables in the pleasant noonday seventy-degree sun, he couldn't believe how quickly his unease had dissipated. After all the numerous preparations, praise *Gott*, everything had fallen into place. And even better than he'd expected.

Abram and Andrew not only delivered the grills, they'd taken over, offering to do all the cooking. He'd caught lots of smiles between grandfather and grandson who seemed to be enjoying their time together.

As promised, Mary Louise dropped off containers of potato salad before trotting off to join her quilting friends and their array of quilts to be auctioned off.

Annie and Rachel, whose ankle was just fine, stood at the third Miller table, which was laden with Annie's delicious baked goods for sale. Katie said that table made sense since dessert was last on most people's list. But he had to smile, knowing Katie probably also liked that the spot was the farthest distance from Andrew.

And then—there was Katie. Standing behind the table next to hers, he glimpsed at her. He saw her ever-present smile as she sincerely thanked an *Englisch* family for making a difference with their purchases. In turn, the family seemed so pleased with the idea that they decided to buy more.

He had to admit, her genuine nature to do good often had that same effect on him too. Overall, he couldn't have handpicked a more dedicated person to partner with even if he'd had the chance to.

Or a prettier one.

The thought came out of nowhere. He blinked. And readily tore his eyes from her. As it was, far beyond Katie being pleasant to look at, he was just thankful that lately having her as his coworker felt easy, uncomplicated.

Then why did I hold onto her hand for so long?

Because…well, he felt sorry for her. That must be it. She was a young widow, and she also had to care for her sister. And, yes, he yearned to know her full story, but he didn't like to pry, especially since he had his own stories he'd prefer not to share.

Feeling somewhat satisfied that he'd come up with an

answer for himself, he bent over the table, straightening plates and napkins that weren't one bit askew.

"Nathan."

Glad for the distraction, he lifted his head to a familiar sounding voice. Instantly, his head jerked. He hadn't realized just how familiar the voice was.

"Moses? What are you doing here?"

"Looking to buy a hot dog, *bruder*."

His brother's smile was the same as always, kind and good-natured. Also, pinched on the right corner of his lip from the disfiguring scar that still covered that side of his face. The scrunched and twisted skin didn't look much less pronounced than it always had. But there was one thing that did look different about Moses. He held a baby boy in his arms.

"But what are you really doing here? Is everything *oll recht*?"

"That's always the first place you go to." His brother chuckled. "Of course, all is fine. Never better in fact." He hugged the infant closer. "Wanted you to meet your new nephew. And I'm still serious about buying a hot dog." He laughed.

Nathan was about to ask Katie to be excused for a few minutes, but he didn't have to. Busy talking to Moses's wife, Celia, and their two-year-old daughter, she'd realized who Moses was. She shooed Nathan away with a flick of her fingers.

Coming from around the table, he gently clasped his brother on the shoulder. "You're not buying anything, *bruder*. For you, the hot dogs are free. It's *verra gut* to see you, but I'm surprised. When I talked to *Mamm* and *Daed* after they visited you in Munfordville, they didn't say anything about you planning to come here."

"It was all last minute. Celia's cousin who lives here—you remember her, right? Elizabeth Haines? She just had a *boppli* recently too, and Celia wanted to come see her. We were going to wait till our little guy was older, but then since you were here, we came now. We didn't want to miss seeing you. Blossom Grove is a lot closer than us trying to get to Middlefield."

"Where are you staying? You can have my room at Happy Endings. I can sleep on a couch there."

"*Danke*, but we're staying at Celia's aunt's house, and we're heading to Celia's sister's house in Adams County tomorrow. Then a driver will take us back home the day after that. All quick visits. But *gut*."

With closed eyes, the baby let out a slight sigh and smacked its lips.

"Anyway, I want you to meet little Nathan."

Nathan? He flinched. "The last time I talked to *Mamm* they were leaving your place and headed to Colorado. She said you hadn't thought of a name yet."

Moses grinned. "She wasn't telling the whole truth."

"I guess not." Nathan shook his head. "I don't understand though. I mean, Nathan Bowman has a *gut* ring to it, for sure. Is Nathan a name Celia liked or something?"

"Nathan, we gave our *buwe* your name to remember the person who saved my life."

Stunned, Nathan took a step back. "That's crazy, Moses. I did no such thing. You almost lost your life because of me," he protested. "I was three years older, and I was supposed to be keeping an eye out for you. Instead, I kept tossing the ball with Levi Fisher as if it was the most important thing in the world to do. At first, I didn't even realize you'd wandered next door. And then when I did—" Remembering what he'd seen, his heart clutched just like it had that day. No way he could finish his sentence.

"Nathan." His brother spoke his name sternly. "You came to my rescue. And how many times do I have to tell you that I hold nothing against you? I was eight years old. The Connors were always burning leaves next door, and I knew better than to get so close to their fires. *Mamm* had told me not to stray there at least a million times. But just as I did get close and tripped, and started to totally fall headfirst into the flames, you were there. You stopped me. You caught me. You rescued me, Nathan."

"It's nice of you to say again, Moses, but—"

His brother interrupted him with a sardonic chuckle. "Oh, Nathan. You need to stop being more scarred from the incident than I am."

Cuddling his infant, Moses dipped his head and took on a serious tone. "Besides, know what I've learned from all of this? I've learned that scars are proof that *Gott* heals. And sometimes, healing comes in many different ways." He angled around to glance where Celia stood with Katie before facing Nathan again. "I'm not saying this about you," his brother continued, "but I think sometimes when a person doesn't forgive themselves or even others, it's an excuse for them not to move on. I know I've done that before in certain matters. But fortunately, Celia changed that about me. Girls are *gut* at getting to the heart of the matter. And to our hearts, period. *Jah*?" He lifted a brow, glancing at the two women again.

Naturally, Nathan found his eyes drawn to the lovely pair, and even more taken in when Katie nodded at him with a smile.

"Now, enough said," Moses spoke.

"Oh, *jah*? You're finally ready to shut your trap?" Even

as Nathan teased, he had to swallow hard. Everything Moses had shared had welled up a mass of emotions that were tough to tamp down.

"I am." Moses chuckled. "And are you ready to say hello to this little *boppli* named after you?" He held out his son to Nathan.

Again, Nathan felt profoundly touched and deeply moved. "I'd be honored to," he replied hoarsely.

His heart did a double beat as Moses settled the child into his outstretched arms. He hadn't held an infant since he'd been on a mission a few years earlier. "Hey there, *boppli buwe*," he cooed to the baby snuggled against his chest. "Hello, little one."

Baby Nathan's eyes fluttered open and stared into space.

"I'm your *onkel*. How do you do?" he said in his softest tone. "Are you liking it here today? We like you." Not receiving any response, he whispered to Moses. "Maybe he doesn't like me. He's not smiling."

"That's because he's too young yet. Generally, at this age, you might see a slight smile when a *boppli* is sleeping. It takes till they're six weeks and more to get a real smile from them."

"You know a lot of babies, Moses."

His brother grinned. "Comes with the territory. You should try it one of these days."

Moses glanced in Katie's direction again, then back at Nathan. His brows were raised, questioning him.

Nathan had no answer for Moses or himself. Instead, he cooed at the *boppli* once again.

Chapter Eleven

"You too?"

Katie practically leaped off the inn's front porch step at the sound of Nathans's voice as he snuck up behind her. Sitting in the quiet, praising *Gott* for His starlit sky and the productive day at the fairgrounds, she certainly hadn't been expecting anyone. Especially so close to midnight.

"I'm sorry," he readily apologized. "I didn't mean to scare you."

"It's *oll recht*. I'm shocked I even had the energy to jump." She chuckled. "After all we did today, we both should be snoozing peacefully."

"I have a feeling you may be like me." He stood, smiling down at her. "Sometimes the more I've done and the more tired I am, I have trouble settling down to sleep." He paused, giving a quick glance at the space on the step beside her. "Mind if I have a seat?"

She slid closer to the handrail to create more room and a proper distance between them. Even so, as Nathan sat down, he didn't seem concerned about that sort of decorum. Instead, he seated himself within a hand's width from her. Near enough that in the glow of the handheld lantern she'd brought outside, his wavy hair appeared even more disheveled than usual. Visible proof, that like her, he'd been in bed tossing and turning. And, she bit back a smile, that wasn't the only thing creating his mussed, masculine look. If he didn't get rid of his days' old facial hair soon, someone may be starting rumors he'd secretly married.

Although come to think of it, she couldn't be looking too good herself. Before coming outside, she'd changed from her nightgown into her wrinkled, stained dress from the day. And now she wished she'd also put her *kapp* back on. But again, she hadn't been expecting company. Feeling self-conscious, she deftly twisted her locks of blond hair into one long strand, leaving it hanging over her shoulder. Aware of Nathan watching her, her cheeks instantly flushed. She rested her hands in her lap and stared into the darkness.

But within moments, the quiet of the night seemed far too still with him sitting beside her. Her mind began swirling all over again just like it had while lying in bed. She tried to think of something to break the silence.

"What a day it was, huh?" She sighed.

"*Jah*, the market made more money for the fund this year than ever before."

"Nathan, more than that happened today." She shot him an incredulous look. "You saved Mildred Hochstetler's life."

"I'd say *Gott* had us do that together, Katie. If you hadn't yelled over at me when I was holding Moses's baby to tell me she was choking on a hot dog, I wouldn't have known."

"And I wouldn't have known how to help her. But you did. I watched you go through it all, step by step."

"I knew what to do from being on the rescue team. But it's not that involved. Anyone can learn."

She started to ask him to teach her. Then recalling how he'd wrapped his arms around Mrs. Hochstetler to save her, a flash of warmth ran up her neck. It was best to put off that lifesaving lesson in broad daylight and with others close by. Not at nighttime, alone. She shivered at the thought.

"Are you cold?" he asked.

"*Nee*, not at all." She shrugged off his concern, turning the attention back to him. "I believe you'll be on Mildred's *gut* list from now on out," she told him. "She was so appreciative. And understandably so. That young *mamm* she was with was so grateful too. That girl had tears in her eyes when she thanked you. But I know it wasn't Mildred's *dochder*. Her daughter's name isn't Sarah. And she's never spoken of this girl before."

"I'm surprised. Mildred never said anything about Sarah…and me?"

"And you? Well, no. Why would she?"

"Because Sarah is Mildred's cousin's *dochder*. And Sarah was the other reason Mrs. Hochstetler isn't too fond of me—besides the tomato incident."

She halfway giggled. "Don't tell me. You took something from Sarah too? What? A watermelon? An apple?"

He gave a wan smile. "If only it'd been that simple." He paused and looked into the moonlit sky, as if searching for something. She knew that feeling well. Moments passed before his eyes sought hers. "Actually, Mildred would say I took Sarah's heart. A lot of people would. I was supposed to marry Sarah. She's the *maedel* I saw at the inn last week when we left in a hurry. The same girl I saw at Bruno's."

"Oh, Nathan." Her hand flew to her mouth. "I'm sorry. I shouldn't have been poking fun."

"Don't feel badly. How could you know?" He looked away, gazing into the night once more. "I couldn't sleep because I kept thinking about how everything I'd been dreading about coming back to Blossom Grove changed today."

With that said, he angled back to her. A thoughtful expression etched his face. "It all came out in the open, and I'm thankful for that."

She had no clue what he was talking about. But she didn't need to prod him into explaining himself. From that moment on, it was as if he needed to tell his story. And she was glad to listen. But it wasn't easy. Watching his range of emotions as he spoke, she found it difficult to keep a handle on her own.

As he talked about the incident with his brother and the fire, her eyes misted. And hearing in his voice how touched he was that Moses named his *boppli buwe* after him, she felt her heart swell. She even nodded understandably as he described how the accident had made him afraid to have *kinner* of his own.

"Because of what happened with Moses," he said so softly she had to strain to hear, "I thought I never wanted *kinner* of my own. I thought... I couldn't be trusted with them."

"Oh, Nathan," she couldn't help herself from saying.

"So I ended up hurting someone else because of my fear. Sarah's family and mine pushed us together, and we...fell into thinking we'd marry. Everyone thought so. But Sarah dreamed of a big family, a whole tribe of *kinner*." At that she heard him utter a wry chuckle.

"I couldn't face that," he admitted. "I went away on a big rescue mission, and then I stayed in Middlefield for months on end. Sarah wrote to me and I wrote back, but eventually I stopped, and, well..."

"She married your friend," she finished for him.

"*Jah*, my best friend. It was a hard reckoning for me. I was happy for them, but...but I couldn't stop wondering if I'd caused her some pain by pretending to be someone I wasn't."

Sitting there, Katie listened to him pour his heart out, and it initiated so many openings in her own. Yet through it all, she kept her hands clenched in her lap. It wasn't easy to do. Especially when she thought of the other closeness that she'd felt with him while holding hands at the market. Another event from the day that had kept her wide-awake.

"And then just the other evening Mary Louise said what I already knew," Nathan continued, looking into her eyes. "Regardless of what anyone thought, I was never supposed to be with Sarah. I only loved her as a friend. Someone I was close to, growing up. As Mary Louise said, I was meant to be with someone else. Katie, I…" He paused. "I'm beginning to think she's right."

His eyes shone tenderly in the light of the pale moon as he gazed at her. Her breath hitched as he slowly and shyly leaned closer. Her pulse quickened as his face and lips were only inches from her own.

Everything inside her said to back away. Even so, she didn't make a move. Not until the inn door suddenly opened behind them. She jolted. He did too.

"Oh, it's you two." Mary Louise put a hand over her heart, appearing thankful. "I got up to get a glass of water and heard voices. I wasn't sure what to think. I'm sorry to interrupt. No need to rush inside." A pleased smile lit the innkeeper's face as she started to close the door.

Instantly, Katie jumped up, relief washing over her— and maybe just a twinge of a letdown too. "No problem. We were just coming in."

"We were?" Nathan questioned her.

"*Jah*, we were. Weren't we?" She shot him a doe-eyed look.

"Uh, *jah, jah*." He blinked. "I guess we were."

As soon as they were inside, it was as if nothing had

taken place during their time under the moonlight. They barely said much of a good-night before going off in opposite directions. Nathan headed to his first-floor bedroom. She climbed the wooden stairs to hers. As she did, she mused. She wasn't sure how she should feel about anything that had happened or been said. There was only one thing she could be certain of. That is, she might've had a hard time falling asleep earlier. Now, she couldn't imagine how she'd catch even a wink before it came time for the sunrise.

Chapter Twelve

"I really will be back as soon as I can, Nathan," Katie said as she grabbed her sweater and handbag from the market's wall rack. "I shouldn't be too long."

"Take your time," he replied. "I won't run the market into the ground while you're gone. I promise."

"Well, if you promise, I guess I can feel safe leaving then." She snickered, donning her light white sweater over her plum-colored dress.

She'd waited until a few days after the fundraiser to schedule an appointment to check out the one-bedroom apartment for rent a half mile from the market. That had given her and Nathan time to get Miller's cleaned up and back on track after the event.

With all their extra busyness in the past week, she hadn't had much time to stew about her apartment hunt. Now, as she strode down the sidewalk toward Periwinkle Lane, everything inside her twittered as her emotions clashed. She felt giddy. Anxious. Gratified. Terrified.

Am I really ready to be doing this? She placed a hand over her roiling stomach. *And why didn't I eat lunch before I left? It might've helped this feeling.*

Yet, she knew no kind of food would've helped quell the tumultuous sensations she was experiencing. And those feelings only intensified as the small studio apartment came into view. Attached to a larger two-story house owned by a Clara Schwartz, the six-hundred-square-foot furnished addition looked tidy and neat from the outside. No doubt it would be plenty big enough for her and Annie on the inside.

But can I do it? Should I do it? Her footsteps faltered. But what else could she do? She couldn't live at Happy Endings forever. And she'd promised herself, *Gott* willing, that she'd work hard to make it on her own. Now that time had come.

Taking a deep breath, she continued placing one foot in front of the other. Until yet another foreboding sensation she knew all too well coursed through her. A tingling warning ran up her neck.

Was it really happening this time? Was she being followed?

Pausing, she glanced cautiously over her shoulder. But there was no one person who stood out. *Englischers* blended with Amish folks dotting the sidewalk behind her.

Clutching her handbag to her side, she scolded herself and kept walking. She was doing it again, wasn't she? Turning her nervous apprehension into something more than what it was. Just like the incident with Nathan's *Englischer* friend. She had to stop. She couldn't keep living her life looking over her shoulder. Or living in the past. She had to concentrate on the here and now. She had to keep moving forward.

As she walked up the porch steps at twenty-six Periwinkle Lane, she kept telling herself that. Even as she stood in the doorway, she couldn't let herself forget. She took a deep breath and smoothed her *kapp*. She turned her worried frown into a friendly smile. She asked *Gott* for His help and mercy. Then she firmly knocked on the door, hoping for the best.

* * *

"Nathan!" Katie placed a hand over her heart as she left the Schwartz home. "What are you doing here? Is something wrong at the market?"

Nathan knew Katie would be surprised to see him waiting for her in a buggy parked outside of the Schwartz house on Periwinkle. But he wasn't prepared for how shocked she looked. That hadn't been his intention when preparing a special outing for her. Or, well, a time for them both to enjoy together, if he were being honest with himself.

"Everything's fine," he tried to assure her. "Hop in."

"Hop in? That's all you have to say?" Her eyes grew even wider.

Ack! This wasn't going so well, was it? He took a deep breath. "How about I help you in?"

"How about you tell me what's going on?" She flung a hand to her hip. "Why aren't you at Miller's? I was just ready to walk back there."

"I'm not at the market because I'm here and you're here, and we're going on an afternoon outing while I have others working the store. There. Is that enough information to get you into this buggy with me?" He knew he'd raised his voice. A few passersby on the sidewalk were proof of that. They'd slowed their pace to frown at him.

"Oh." Her forehead creased, still looking puzzled. "And where is this outing?"

"Katie Troyer, for once can you just trust me?"

She hesitated before stepping up into the buggy. Once she got settled, he thought it best to give her the bag of items he'd purchased over a week ago. Maybe that would get them off on the right foot.

"Here, I got a little something for you."

Her brows furrowed once more as she peered into the bag. "Drawing paper, pencils and colored pencils?"

"*Jah*. You may want to have them once we get to where we're going."

"Now you've really got me wondering."

Finally. A curious smile curled her lips and lit her eyes. It was just the reaction he'd initially been hoping for. Grinning, he tapped the reins to get Rusty moving toward their destination.

"What did you think of Clara Schwartz's apartment?" he asked once they were farther down the road.

"You know her?"

"*Jah*. She's a nice woman and has a *gut* reputation for keeping up her place."

"That's good to hear. I thought she seemed that way too." She hesitated. "I have to give her an answer in the next couple of days. But I just don't know."

"Is the apartment too small for you?"

"Oh, *nee*. It's fine, better than fine for Annie and me." She hugged the bag to her chest as she looked at him. "It's just what if something happens and I can't make the payments? What if I'm biting off more than I can chew? What if Annie feels more lost without being around Mary Louise each day? What if I can't do this?"

He couldn't fault her for thinking that way. Hadn't he been doing the same thing ever since she'd graced him with her smile? Asking himself, what if he decided to stay in Blossom Grove? What if he never returned to Middlefield? What if he told her how much he'd been thinking of her lately? And what if now, seeing the distress in her expression, he bent toward her and kissed her rosy cheek to calm her? Because that's what he wanted to do.

"Nathan, what are you staring at?"

"Huh?" Her voice jolted him.

"You were staring at me. Is there something on my face?" Freeing a hand, she brushed at the same cheek he'd been considering kissing. "Or on my *kapp*?" She ducked her head for him to see better.

"*Nee*. Not at all." He cleared his throat, straightening in his seat. "I, uh, I was just thinking that life is full of what-ifs. But, Katie, you're..." Looking over at her, his thoughts jumbled. What could he say? That she was beautiful. A real catch. The sweetest girl he ever met. Smart. That was it. He needed to stick with the latter. "Katie, you're smart and whatever you put your mind to, you can do. I know because I've seen that in you."

"You really think so?" she asked in a soft voice.

"I know so." He nodded.

She sighed. "*Danke*, Nathan." Reaching over, she placed a thankful hand lightly on his forearm. He patted it reassuringly, removing his fingers quickly. Fortunately, she did the same.

"And, to put your mind totally at ease before we reach our destination," he told her, "you should know that the market is in good hands from now till closing. I forgot that Barbara Glick's sister Celeste worked at the store forever ago. Both of those ladies are there for the afternoon with Sylvia who appreciated having an excuse to get out of the house for a few hours. Annie and Mary Louise said they'd pop in too, to see if the women needed any help."

He thought he'd done a great job of planning, yet there sat Katie shaking her head at him.

"Katie, I promised you earlier that the market wouldn't fall apart today, and it won't. Everything will be fine."

"It's not that, Nathan. I just can't believe you organized all of that without me knowing."

Obviously touched, her eyes gazed at him with grati- tude. "Oh, well…" He shrugged as if setting everything up had been nothing. "Isn't that what a surprise is all about?"

Her appreciation was still stirring him in a good way ten minutes later as the buggy approached the Park at Almond Creek. Seeing the sign, Katie gasped out loud.

"Nathan!" She grasped his arm again. "I've always wanted to come here. How did you know?"

The truth was he hadn't. He simply had wanted to take her to a place where she could see all the exotic animals she hadn't seen in her backyard—or anywhere else. And, well, he did want to make her happy as well. Because as selfish as it was, lately he noticed that witnessing the sparkle in her eyes and a sweet smile on her face did something for him. It made him happy too. And when was the last time that happened with a girl? He'd racked his brain and ques- tioned his heart. Still, he truly couldn't remember.

As he pulled into the animal park, his lightheartedness did wane some, remembering that tomorrow he and Katie would be back to business. Not only that, in less than ten days, he'd no longer be working, riding, eating, enjoying a starlit night's sky or an afternoon outing by her side. Thank- fully, Katie's excitement jarred those dismal thoughts.

"Nathan," she exclaimed. "There's a giraffe." She pointed in the distance. "I've never ever seen one in person. Oh, they really are so tall." She declared in astonishment. "What a wonder it is!"

Watching an amazed expression light her face, he had a wonder of his own. Something he couldn't quit marvel- ing about. That is, how had the time in Blossom Grove that he thought would never end go by so quickly? Far too quickly for him.

Chapter Thirteen

❧

Katie was thrilled when Nathan suggested Almond Creek's horse-drawn wagon ride as the best way to see the entire park and handfeed the creatures residing there. As the driver halted the cart filled with other park visitors yet again, Katie leaned over the wagon's metal side rail once more too. This time it was to offer a huge Brahman cow a snack from the last of the two feed buckets Nathan had purchased.

"You really like animals of all sizes, don't you?" Nathan chuckled.

"I do. *Gott*'s creatures are magnificent, ain't so?"

She'd been awed by all she'd seen from the moment they'd joined others on the wagon ride. The park hosted hundreds of animals from six of the seven continents. The opportunity to get so close and actually feed many of the exotic animals along with more common ones overwhelmed her. She didn't know if Nathan had noticed. But a couple of times throughout the ride, she'd been so moved by it all, she'd had to blink back tears.

"There's an ostrich that nobody's noticed venturing over to the back of the wagon," she informed Nathan. "Just in case you want to feed it."

"I would absolutely do that." He smiled. "If someone hadn't taken my bucket of feed when theirs ran out."

"Oh, I guess I did do that, didn't I?" She bit her lip. "Want it back?"

"Nee." He laughed. "It's just as enjoyable—even more fun—watching you give out treats."

She had to admit she couldn't have been happier for him to say so. Especially since a group of the most adorable spotted fawns several yards away appeared to be waiting patiently for goodies from everyone. Besides that, she could tell their forty-five-minute wagon ride was coming closer to an end. A little way up ahead, she could spy the place where they'd first boarded the cart.

But after visiting with the fawns, she tried not to look at the end in sight as the wagon bumped over the grassy terrain. Because their last stop brought the wagon to other creatures she'd never seen in person before—a family of kangaroos.

Taking her turn behind a few others, she offered the smallest of that clan the chance to gobble down the remaining morsels from her, well, Nathan's bucket. That done, she swiveled back around in her seat and sighed. Nathan gave her an appraising smile.

"I think that kangaroo liked you."

"Do you think it may want to come home with me?"

He laughed. "I wouldn't doubt it. But Mary Louise may have something to say about that."

"Annie too, when I give that cute 'roo her bed." She giggled.

Once the driver started up the wagon again, there was no question they were headed back to the starting spot. But as much as Katie tried to soak in the last of the beautiful scenery, suddenly she couldn't. All at once, she was too aware of Nathan. Too mindful of his arm casually stretched out on the railing behind her. The gesture wasn't in any way an embrace. Yet, that closeness of him felt so natural and protective, like nothing she could remember. Trying not to let herself feel that way, she surreptitiously inched up to the edge of the seat. Or so she thought. Apparently, she hadn't been so discreet. Nathan noticed.

"Anxious to be the first one out of the wagon?" he asked.

"*Nee*, I just—"

Before she could finish the sentence—or make up whatever story she needed to cover her feelings—the driver shouted whoa. The horses and wagon came to an abrupt stop. Unfortunately, she didn't. Jolted, her body began to fly off the rim of the seat. Just then the arm she'd worked to distance herself from caught her from behind. With two arms, Nathan fully embraced her.

"You *oll recht*?" His gaze was concerned as he looked down at her. His caress just as comfortable and safe as she'd imagined. The warmth of it heated her cheeks, which embarrassed her even more.

"I'm fine. *Danke*." She met his gaze. "Just got caught off balance." *In more ways than one*, she thought.

Thankfully, the driver's voice rang out, interrupting the awkward moment. "I hope everyone had an enjoyable time today," he announced. "Be sure to leave your empty buckets up here by me."

As riders began to shuffle to their feet, Nathan loosened his grasp. She willingly wiggled from his arms, dutifully gathering up their buckets. After turning them in and thanking the driver, she descended the wagon with Nathan behind her. She was just about to also thank him for a wonderful time when he spoke up.

"I have one more thing here that I'd like to show you."

"Another animal?" She couldn't imagine.

"Eh, yes and no. Not exactly. But the place is a bit of a walk to get to," he warned.

From the expression on his face, he appeared so excited she couldn't refuse his enthusiasm. "I'm okay with that," she agreed.

It didn't take long for her to realize that Nathan hadn't exaggerated. Together, they traipsed over an open field. Stopped momentarily to appreciate the Almond Creek itself and its lovely miniature waterfall. After that, they panted— she more than Nathan—up countless stone steps. When they finally reached the top of that hill, Katie knew they'd arrived at their destination. There, they were welcomed by a sizeable wooden porch swing hanging from sturdy metal bars sunken into a small concrete foundation. Surrounded by trees, the swing was set apart, nestled in silence. Yet, everything the park had to offer could be seen below like a mural stretched out on a canvas.

"Nathan, this is amazing!" She gasped.

"I'm just glad the swing is empty, and no one else is up here."

"*Jah*, that is *gut*. Though I still would've loved seeing this view even for a second."

"Well, seems like we have more time than that now. Want to have a seat?" Nathan held onto the swing's arm while she sat down. Then he settled in beside her. After barely a minute, he turned to her.

"I was just thinking. We should've gotten the art supplies from the buggy before we came up here, so you could relax and sketch. I'm happy to go get them," he offered.

"That's *verra* nice of you, Nathan. And I thank you so much for buying those things for me. But for right now, I'm fine just taking in everything there is to see. And I'll never forget all I've already seen either. I know I'll be using the paper and pencils to sketch it all in the future."

"Are you saying it's been better than seeing those animals in a book?" He quirked a hopeful brow.

"So much better I can't describe it. To get an actual feel of what those creatures are all about has been *wunderbaar.* Now they're ingrained in my memory in a special way." And in her heart, she didn't add. Just like the man who'd brought her to see them.

"We'll bring Annie the next time we come. She'd like to meet the animals, wouldn't she?"

"My *schweschder*?" Katie smiled. "She may stay and live with them."

It was a sweet thought on Nathan's part to include Annie. But he had to know as she did that it was just that. He'd already stopped wearing his splint regularly, which meant there wasn't much time left before he was leaving. And things were likely to get busier at the market in the final days.

But at one point in the future, she promised herself she would bring her sister. Even though she knew when that day came, it would be filled with memories of Nathan and the here and now.

By that time would she still be overcome by all that she was feeling now?

Because sitting next to the person whose thoughtfulness had brought her to this place…feeling a sense of peace she hadn't experienced in years and years…gratitude welled up inside her. Tears sprung to her eyes as she looked over at him. Yet, a twinge of sorrow clutched her heart too. Oh, how she was going to miss him! The inherent strength in his face. The touches of humor around his mouth and eyes.

So, so different from arrogant Jonathan. Nathan had no idea how naturally handsome he was. Nor did he seem to care.

"Now you're looking at me funny," he said. "Do I have something on my face? Or on my hat?" He took off the straw hat and ruffled his light brown hair.

"*Nee*…it's just…" She paused, attempting to get a hold of her emotions. "Nathan, I can't thank you enough for bringing me here today. No one has done anything like this for me since…" Her voice grew hoarse. "I don't even remember when. I just know it's been a long, long time since I've enjoyed something so much."

"Aw. You deserve it, Katie. You work so hard. And do so much for the market. For your sister. For me."

"For *you*?" She swiped a tear from the corner of her eye.

"*Jah*, you, uh. ." he stuttered. "You make me feel like I belong here again."

"But you do belong, Nathan," she countered. "Blossom Grove is your hometown. You grew up here."

"True." He lifted his chin. His blue eyes shone intensely as he focused on hers. "But somehow, Katie, it's you that makes it feel like home."

She knew what a glimmer of appreciation was. She'd caught that look plenty from satisfied customers. But the way Nathan gazed at her, she saw a fondness she'd never witnessed in the eyes of any man. And she felt it too. Her breath quickened. Her cheeks flushed with warmth. And her heart took note, fluttering in her chest.

Yet as much as she didn't want to, she had to glance away from his gaze.

Don't! Don't be drawn in. You promised you're going by the book, not by your heart. You need to protect yourself and most of all, Annie.

"Katie." The softness in Nathan's voice drew her back to him. "I'm sorry. Did I say too much?"

"*Nee*. Not at all," she replied readily. Even so, it was taking a moment to gather her emotions and thoughts. "I mean, I can say the same of you, Nathan. You've made the town more like home to me. And for Annie too. She really likes and respects you. She thinks of you as a *gut* friend. And I—I do too."

She hated how his mouth opened slightly and his head dipped, as if that may have been disappointing to hear. But she needed to stress their friend relationship as much for him as for herself.

"Well…" he said after some seconds. She noticed him swallow hard. "You Troyer *maedels* are hard not to like. You're both funny, cute, nice and talented."

Instantly, she took a chance. Jumping in on his last word, she hoped to lighten both of their moods again.

"Talented? Oh, now I see. Is that why you brought me to Almond Creek?"

She punched his shoulder, kiddingly. And was glad to get a chuckle out of him as he rubbed his upper arm.

"That was a *verra* quick change of subject, Miss Troyer. I have no idea what you're talking about."

"Uh-huh. Sure." She narrowed her eyes at him, teasingly. "It's all about the market's sidewalk chalkboard, isn't it?"

"Again, I don't understand."

"Really? Because I'm pretty sure and certain that I know what you're thinking."

"Oh, *jah*?" He blinked, appearing equally confused and amused. "Please tell me."

"You want to see more exotic animals on the sidewalk board, don't you? Like a drawing of a kangaroo with the words *hop on in for special treats.* Or *jump inside for our fruit specials today.*"

He laughed, which kept her going.

"Or, if you want, I can always draw giraffes with a different message."

"Oh, yeah. Like what?"

"I don't know." She shrugged. "Something like 'Miller's Market is tall on savings.' Or 'come in for giant savings today.'"

"That's a *gut* one too." He grinned. "You're a natural, Katie."

Natural. She swayed in her seat, hearing him use the same word that had been in her mind about him all along. Because more and more, that's how right and good and easy it felt to be around him.

As they rocked gently in the swing, she looked out at the expanse of *Gott*'s creation and creatures. And couldn't keep herself from questioning Him.

Why couldn't You have let me meet Nathan earlier in my life, Lord? At a time when my heart—and world—hadn't yet been torn apart. When it still made sense to be open to love...

On the ride back from Almond Creek, a slight evening breeze whispered its way around the buggy. Because of that, Nathan retrieved a shawl, most likely one of Mary Louise's, from the back seat. Offering it to Katie, she'd been happy to wrap it over her light sweater. Every time that he glanced in her direction, he couldn't help but notice how cozy she appeared. Or how the purple color of the knitted shawl highlighted her blond hair even more. To his eyes, she looked fetching in general. That was true even when he caught her in the middle of a yawn.

"It's been a big day for you, hasn't it? Seeing the apartment and the park?"

"Jah." She rubbed the corner of her eye. "I don't think I'll have any trouble sleeping tonight."

"Well, you can get settled in soon. We're almost back home," he assured her. "I mean back to the inn." He corrected himself.

"I knew what you meant." She gave him a slight grin before yawning again.

After rounding two more corners and listening to several more minutes of Rusty's clip-clopping, he could see Happy Endings come into view. Washed in the glow of the soon-to-be sunset, the place looked just as enchanting as it did by day.

"I wonder whose car is sitting in front of the inn?" Katie sat up straighter, presumably to get a better look.

"Maybe it's someone who stopped to get information about booking Happy Endings," he suggested. "Or Mary Louise does have plenty of *Englisch* and Mennonite friends who could be paying her a visit."

"True." She nodded.

"How about I drop you off out front? Then I'll go take care of Rusty and the buggy."

"That sounds *gut*."

With that, Katie began gathering up her purse, the bag of art supplies and plenty of Almond Creek brochures she'd brought along. She'd mentioned that she wanted to display the pamphlets in the market, which was fine with him. It was more proof she'd enjoyed their time at the park and that couldn't have made him happier.

Well, that wasn't exactly true. Glancing at her charming profile, he knew that if he'd heard that she thought of him as more than a friend, the day would've been even more special.

As it was, he had a hard time hiding his disappointment. Though he'd been more than pleased to see her reaction to the park visit, he had to admit he'd hoped the excursion would have resulted in a deepening of their relationship.

There was no denying he was falling for Katie as more than a friend. He wanted to get to know her better, even possibly court her.

Yes, court her. Just thinking the words brought him up short. When had he started thinking in those terms?

No matter. She clearly still clung to the grief of her widowhood and wasn't ready to think of courting anyone, let alone him.

He sighed and tugged on the reins, bringing Rusty and the buggy to a halt a safe distance behind the car.

"Sure you don't need any help with those things?" He nodded at the items in Katie's arms.

"*Nee, danke*. I can manage."

Even with her hands full, Katie daintily slipped out of the buggy. But just as she did, Nathan noticed more movement. Up ahead, a man exited the gray vehicle parked close by. With long strides, the stranger approached the sidewalk swiftly.

It was all so odd to watch…the man…the timing…the determined steps—toward Katie.

All at once, adrenaline shot through him. He jumped out of the buggy. With an even faster pace, he rushed to stand next to her. A need to protect her surged through his veins.

The dark-haired stranger barely glimpsed at him. Instead, the man's wide eyes were riveted on Katie.

"You're Katie. Right?" the man asked.

Katie's head jerked at the sound of her name, making

it clear she'd been caught off guard. Seeing her that way, Nathan's jaw instantly clenched. He braced his shoulders, ready to do whatever was needed to keep her safe. He moved closer to her side.

"Did I see you—" she stammered and Nathan watched her eyes narrow. "Were you..." Her voice trembled with fear. "Did you follow me today?"

Before the man even answered, as if she'd solved a horrible answer to a puzzle, Nathan sensed her freeze. Knowing how scared she seemed, he took a step closer to the man.

Still, the stranger ignored him.

"You may have," the man answered. "I saw you had things to do. I thought I'd wait to come to you now."

No words came from Katie's mouth. She tilted her head, looking as frightened as she was confused.

"You do look familiar," she murmured. "But you can't. There's no way. I don't know you."

The man shifted on his feet. "Maybe I look familiar because people say I resemble my brother."

"Your brother?" Katie frowned.

"Yes. Your deceased husband. I'm Peter Lantz."

Katie's mouth dropped open, and her body rocked. She lost her step and staggered. Nathan wasn't completely clear why hearing that name could knock her off her feet. He was only thankful to *Gott* he could be there to catch her. Holding her close to him, he wished he could protect her from whatever she was feeling. Not just in this instance... but always.

Chapter Fourteen

"**I** think it'd be better if you left, Mr. Lantz."

Completely dazed by what had just occurred, Katie was also taken aback by Nathan's voice. As she stood wrapped in the security of his arms, his tone was unlike anything she'd heard from him before. Stern. Unfriendly. Foreign to her ears. She also caught Peter's reply.

"I'm not here to hurt anyone. Believe me."

Believe him? Oh, how familiar were those words? She'd heard them spew from Jonathan's mouth plenty. So many times, that the sound of them still sickened her stomach. Yet it was enough to revive her too.

As safe as it felt to be so close to Nathan, she immediately wriggled from his embrace. *Gott* forgive her, but she couldn't help from lashing out at the man standing before her.

"I should trust that coming from a person named Lantz? How can you be serious?"

The man rubbed his forehead. Then looked away as if searching the sunset for the right thing to say. "Please." He turned back to her. "Please, can I have a few minutes of your time? Just a few minutes to talk?" He glimpsed at Nathan, then back to her. "Alone?"

Her heart hadn't stopped its frantic beat. Her hands were

clenched into fists as if she could fight off what had taken place in the past and what was happening now. Why was this man here at all? It made no sense.

"I'd appreciate it," Peter Lantz added. "Ten minutes. That's all I ask." He tilted his head, awaiting her response.

She was sure there was nothing he could say to change the way that his brother had taken everything from her and Annie. Their family's house…a home filled with so many memories…their security…and trust.

But she had noticed the Florida license plate on the gray sedan. At some point, had Peter Lantz really driven thirteen hours or more to get to Ohio? If that was the case, should she give him what he asked for?

It was her turn to stare off into the distance, seeking out an answer. As much as she didn't want to give in to him, she caved.

"Fine." Like Nathan's voice, her own sounded alien as she practically spat out the word. Then she turned to Nathan. His expression was filled with the utmost concern. "I'll be *oll recht*, Nathan. You can go get Rusty settled in."

Even with that said, Nathan didn't move an inch. His caring touched her to the depths of her heart. Something she so needed in that moment.

"Truly, Nathan. It's okay."

He took a moment to search her eyes. Then inhaling a deep breath, he nodded. "I'll be close by. Right over there." He pointed toward Rusty's stable area. She knew he was saying so more for the man's benefit than hers. That seemed particularly true when she watched him glower at the former brother-in-law that she never knew she had.

"You'd better not hurt her," Nathan warned Peter, his jaws visibly clenched.

"That's not my intention at all," Peter replied softly.

Before taking his leave, Nathan picked up her purse and parcels that had gotten tossed and scattered on the ground. With nothing else to concern her except the man in front of her, she crossed her arms over her chest.

"Do you want to sit up on the porch?" Peter Lantz asked.

She glanced up and saw both Annie and Mary Louise peering out the inn's open screened-in window. "Did you already go in and ask for me?"

"I did."

Surely, that meant Annie and Mary Louise were beyond curious. Yet, she didn't want to be close enough that they may overhear whatever he might have to say.

"I'd rather we stand right where we are." True, her legs hadn't stopped trembling. But surely, she could manage to dig her feet solidly into the ground for ten minutes. Couldn't she? "I don't know why you came all this way, Mr. Lantz. I have nothing left to give. Your *bruder* took it all from us. Everything."

"I presumed that," he replied solemnly. "And, I want you to know that the other members in the Lantz family are very sorry. We aren't like my brother."

"That's *gut*. Because hopefully, the rest of you aren't out there taking advantage of a woman like me. They aren't pretending to be someone they're not. And they're not stealing from families with no regard for who they're hurting." Emotion welled up in her throat. She worked to swallow it away, though not so successfully. Moisture misted her eyes.

"No, we're not." He dipped his chin. "And I can say I'm sorry for what Jonathan did to you again and again. But that doesn't change the fact that he had a gambling addiction and he abused your trust."

"Ha! That's not even the half of it. When we married, I

turned the deed of the house over to him. It was the wifely thing to do."

"Let me guess," Peter spoke up. "In the end—his end—he'd lost your house because of his gambling habits and debts."

She nodded. "Not only that, before we had to move out, there were random men who came knocking on our door. People he owed money to. I don't even know how they found me. But to this day, I'm still afraid. Still fearful of being followed."

"I can imagine."

"No," she retorted, her voice heightening. "You may say that. But, no, you can't imagine. You can't know how helpless I felt trying to protect my sister. Or how sad it was to have to take her away from the only home, the only life and people she knew. But what else could I do? We needed a fresh start. A place to try and build a life again. And then you come here—and why? Why remind us of all of it again? It's not like it ever leaves me anyway." She paused, realizing she was glaring at him. "Every day I keep praying. Praying I can forgive Jonathan. Along with that other woman."

"The other woman?" Peter frowned. "Do you mean Tricia Hargraves?"

The woman's name would forever be etched in her memory. So would the hour that Karen Brenner, her *Englisch* next-door neighbor back in Tuscarawas County rushed over to her house with a local newspaper. Karen had been in the habit of letting her papers pile up, and just happened to look at a two-day old paper with a photo of Jonathan on the front page. But it wasn't the Jonathan she knew—not the Amish man that Katie thought she'd married. Or the man she'd introduced her neighbor to. It was Jonathan, an *Englischer*, who'd been killed in a car accident in a vehicle that he'd been driving. Along with him in the car was another woman, Tricia Hargraves, and her son, Max. The two of them had been injured but both survived.

"*Jah*, that woman," she answered Peter. "The woman who I'm sure benefited from Jonathan tricking me."

Katie's stomach roiled, remembering how hard it had been to look at those photos. Not just the shock of reading that Jonathan had died in the crash. But seeing the other woman, visualizing his other life. And then, all at once, so many things had started to make sense to her. Like why he'd said the only job he could find was working at an Amish company in a neighboring town. Like why he'd pretended to be working so hard that she wouldn't see him for weeks on end. And, even why he insisted on having some of their mail and statements go to a post office box in that town to save her from being bothered with it. He'd lied and lied some more, which crushed her. But she'd also cried countless tears, wondering how a woman could also do such a thing to another female.

"No, no," Peter waved a hand in the air.

"No, what?"

"That's not how it was at all. Sadly, Jonathan did the same thing to Tricia who happened to be a single widowed mother. She told me she was naive enough to think he really cared about her and her son. When Jonathan pretended to be using her savings and her husband's death benefits to make investments for her future, she believed him. And didn't question him. Obviously, the only thing he was investing in was his gambling."

Katie rocked on her feet, her head swimming. Would *Gott* ever forgive her for judging someone so wrongly?

"Like you," Peter continued, "she's had to move on. She and Max are now living with her sister in Missouri until she gets back on her feet. But she gave me something that she thought someone may like to have. I believe that someone is you."

Katie stared at him blankly as he pulled a book from the leather satchel looped over his shoulder. "This belongs to you, Katie. To your family."

She recognized the book the moment he held it out to her. Taking it from his grasp, she hugged it to her chest. Tears began to trickle down her cheeks.

"It was my father's," she uttered throatily. "My *daed*'s Bible."

Her mother had been in her last months before going to be with the Lord when Jonathan showed up at their house. He was all decked out in men's Amish clothing and had their language down pat. Hearing that he was searching for handyman jobs, Katie had been happy to hire him. There'd been plenty to do since her father had passed the year before. Ultimately, her *mamm* had been just as fooled by Jonathan appearing Amish as she was.

"When Jonathan asked to marry me, my *mamm* insisted he have our father's Bible." She sniffled. "I can't believe I have this in my hands again."

"Tricia found it in one of Jonathan's suitcases at her house and realized it wasn't his. She also never saw him open it."

"I wonder if it would've helped if he had," she said quietly.

"I guess we'll never know, will we? At least it led me to you."

"I've been wondering this whole time how you found me."

"I saw the name and address on the inside front cover

of the Bible. I drove there and realized you'd moved out. So, I went to your neighbor's."

"You met Karen?"

He nodded. "She was hesitant and cautious. She wanted to take the Bible and mail it to you herself. But I…" He took a deep breath. "It took much convincing, but I explained how coming here myself might offer some closure for you—and for my family too. I thought it would mean more if I could say how sorry we are in person. So, she described you and said I could find you here. She knew how much it would mean to you to have at least that part of your family back again." He paused. "Katie, we don't have much money to give to you—"

She held up her hand to stop him. "And I don't want any. What happened is not your fault."

"Well, I at least wanted to bring the Bible and I wanted to say I'm sorry. In person. So—" He clapped his hands together and took a deep breath. "Now that I've done that, I best get going."

"Do you want to come in for a cup of tea first?" she asked politely, not even sure why the offer slipped from her lips.

Peter looked up at the window where Annie and Mary Louise were still standing. Then she noticed him peer over her shoulder. She turned and saw Nathan within hearing range. Had he been there all along?

"Thank you, but I think you have some people who are waiting for you."

"*Jah*, I do," she replied, feeling a wave of thankfulness fill her heart.

But just as Peter departed and Nathan came to her side, that sensation quickly disappeared. Apprehension took its place, knowing questions would be asked.

"Are you okay, Katie?"

That wasn't the first question she'd been expecting. She thought he'd be asking what Peter's visit was all about. Or about the Bible she was holding in her hand. But no, he'd asked about her. His concern was for her alone.

So touched by his thoughtfulness, she felt her mouth begin to quiver. So overcome by his caring, she felt her eyes brim with tears without warning. Then, thinking of all she'd been through…and how no man had ever been so unselfishly kind to her…those tears flooded her cheeks.

Weeping uncontrollably, she couldn't manage to verbally answer him. She merely nodded that she was all right. But Nathan knew better. In fact, he seemed to know exactly what she needed. He opened his arms and she fell into them, hugging the Bible close to her chest. Nestled against the warmth of him, she cried tear after tear. Tears she hadn't even known she'd been holding inside.

Chapter Fifteen

"Schweschder!"

Katie backed away from Nathan's caress at the sound of Annie's voice. She rubbed frantically at her cheeks, hoping to hide the wetness as Annie came running down the porch steps.

"Who was that? What's going on? Do we have to leave this town too?"

Hearing the trembling fear in Annie's tone was awful enough. But also seeing the stark sadness in her sister's expression was heartbreaking. It was like nothing Katie had witnessed in a while. And then so quickly there it was, all back again. Her chest ached, wanting to erase it in a second.

"Leave here? Oh, Annie, Annie...*nee, nee*..." Holding the Bible in one arm, she pulled Annie close with her other. "It's nothing like that."

She glanced over Annie's shoulder at Nathan, still not sure what all he'd heard. But he didn't seem as concerned about what had gone on with Peter as much as with her and Annie. In fact, he tilted his head toward Annie as if signaling he knew that she needed to be Katie's primary focus. Then graciously, he took another step back.

"If either of you need me, I'll be inside." His offer came with a smile that was slight but encouraging. As he strode away, she had to wonder about the lines at the corners of his eyes. Were they as much about humor as from him narrowing his vision to see into the needs of others?

Her musing was instantly interrupted by Annie, who'd backed out of her hug. And rightfully so. Unfortunately, her sister's curiosity couldn't be contained any longer.

"Who was the man that came, Katie? And don't lie." Her sister peered at her.

"Lie?" Katie felt her neck stiffen. "When have I ever lied to you?"

"Well, maybe not lie exactly. But don't leave anything out like you do sometimes. Often, in fact."

Katie couldn't argue about that even if she wanted to. No doubt, Annie could accuse her of doing just that.

"The man you saw is named Peter."

"So?" Annie shrugged and her forehead furrowed.

There was no easy way to deliver the news, just as it hadn't been easy for her to hear it either. Inhaling deeply, Katie had to force herself to say more. "He's Peter Lantz, Annie. Jonathan's brother."

The heavy lashes that shadowed Annie's cheeks shot up. Her hand flew to her lips. "No, no, no. Not another one of them."

Katie grasped her sister's hand and gently squeezed it in her own. "Annie." She looked her sister in the eye. "Don't you worry. There's nothing to be afraid of. He came to give us this." She held out the Bible to her sister. All at once, a spark of happiness lit her heart being able to share the next words. "It's *Daed*'s, Annie. It's our father's."

Annie's eyes grew even wider, instantly glistening with emotion. Katie completely understood. She'd had the same reaction. "And I'm giving it to you, *schweschder*. It's yours to keep now."

Annie took the holy book from her hand. At once, she gently, almost reverently, opened the cover. Seeing their father's name written there, she ran her hand over the inked impression that had existed for decades before either of them had even been born.

Her sister's expression was pleased but puzzled as she looked back up at Katie. "I don't understand. How did the brother find the Bible? And us?"

Katie took a deep breath. After letting it out slowly, she bit her lip. What to tell? What not to say? Her mind kept flitting back and forth.

"Katie, whatever the story is, you don't have to hold back from me. I never liked Jonathan Lantz from the first time I met him."

Katie's head jerked. Once again, she was taken aback by how her younger sister had been better at reading him than she'd been. "You didn't like him at all?"

"No. I even told Mary Louise that about him. And I told her some other things about him too."

Katie winced in reply.

"I'm sorry, Katie. But I had to tell someone. Maybe you thought he'd be *gut* for us. But I saw how sad you were when he was never around—and even when he was." She paused. "And I don't know the details, but I know it had to be his fault that we had to up and move. I saw the newspaper. He wasn't Amish at all."

"Annie, I had no idea you saw the paper. You never said anything." Her knees grew weak, thinking of the heaviness her sister must've been carrying around for so long. "I'm so sorry. So *verra* sorry, Annie. I thought I'd hidden everything from you."

"I know you were only trying to protect me. Because that's what you always do. You catch me so I won't fall down the stairs. And you're there to lift me up when I do fall. But, Katie, that's got to stop some. You can't protect me from life—from everything. So, please tell me," Annie cried to her. "Tell me all of it. I'm ready to hear."

"Oh, Annie." She sighed, wondering how to explain everything in the briefest way possible. "Jonathan Lantz... well...he was a man who gave in to temptation. That's all. He fell prey to many temptations."

"Really, Katie?" her sister huffed. "You can't believe that's enough for me to hear, do you? You sound like a minister."

She'd hoped her succinct version of the story would suffice. But obviously, Annie wasn't having it. Could she really blame her?

"Just be my sister and tell me. Won't you, please?" Annie continued to beg. "I don't want to spend my whole life wondering."

Hearing the hoarseness in her sister's voice...watching her clutch the Bible like the lifeline it was... Katie's heart softened even more. She'd had the chance to learn more from Peter today. And hadn't it helped to put the unforgiveness behind? Hadn't it helped to release so many unshed tears?

"You're right, Annie. You deserve more than that," she conceded. "Let's go sit on the porch and talk. I'll tell you everything."

With that, Annie's face lit up with relief. Probably just knowing she didn't have to plead anymore to learn the details of how their lives had been turned upside down was enough to brighten her expression. Yet Katie didn't expect her sister's eyes to still be sparkling when she'd finished explaining the entire Jonathan story. Even so, if the two of them were ever going to put the past behind them, then sharing all with her sister was the right thing to do. Because as Annie grabbed her hand and began to lead their way to the porch, it came to Katie. They were family. The only family they had. And together was the way it should be. Together was far better.

Nathan knew Katie needed space. But all throughout a quiet dinner with the four of them seated around Mary Louise's table, it wasn't easy to give her.

Nor could he forget about her soon after supper when she retreated with Annie to their upstairs bedroom.

How was she doing? What was she feeling?

The wondering had him all keyed up. Hoping to ease his restlessness, he settled in the calm of the sitting room. But after reading the mail Mary Louise had given him, he only felt even more tightly wound. Laying the envelopes atop the side table, he reached for a book sitting there instead. Yet even though his eyes scanned the words on the pages, he had no clue where the story was going. Parts of the conversation he'd overheard between Katie and her former brother-in-law kept unsettling him, leaving his thoughts spinning even more.

All along he'd assumed Katie's reluctance to be more than friends was rooted in her grief over losing her husband. Now, however, it seemed as if her husband had created problems that still haunted her. Knowing that, his heart swelled with sympathy all over again. But alongside that came a feeling he couldn't control. A rush of anger filled him too. Anger at any man who would treat such a sweet woman with anything but respect and love.

If only he could hold her in his arms again and hug away all that had happened to her. More than he even knew. Yet, she hadn't approached him again since their earlier embrace. So, what could he possibly do?

Just go to bed. Be done with the day, he told himself, snapping the book shut.

"Nathan?"

Even just the hush of Katie saying his name felt like a salve to him.

"I didn't hear you come down the stairs." Because he'd been too caught up listening to all the questions shooting through his mind?

"I tiptoed," she replied. "Annie's asleep with the Bible under her pillow."

"That sounds like a good place for it to be." He smiled.

"*Jah*, it is." There was a peacefulness to her timbre. But it only lasted a moment. "Nathan, do you, um…do you have a minute?" she asked, rubbing her hands together.

"As many minutes as you'd like."

"Want to go outside?" She raised a hopeful brow.

Even to him, fresh evening air sounded good. As he let her lead the way to the bench in the garden, it felt that way too. Plus, the whimsical memory of planting celery with her flitted through his mind as they sat down, side by side.

"Well, here we are," he uttered just for something to say.

"*Jah*, here we are," she repeated, looking over at him. "Nathan, I… You…" she stuttered.

Realizing how nervous she was, he placed a hand over hers. "Katie, it's fine. You don't have to say anything if you don't want to. We're out here with *Gott* working all around us. The stars are bright. The moon is pale. There's a slight breeze. And I'm just happy to be out here…with you."

"But I do have to say something." She slid her hand out from under his. "Nathan, I want to be honest with you."

"I appreciate that, Katie. But if it's about what happened

with you and your husband, don't feel like you have to share. Not unless you want to."

Of course, he wanted to hear her story, to know everything the woman he cared so much for had gone through. Even so, if it only placed more stress or pain on her shoulders for telling it, for her sake, he could deal without knowing too.

She gave him a long look, then nodded. "I do want to share."

Watching her as she spoke, seeing the wholesome prettiness of her features and knowing the sweetness that existed inside her, he was taken aback. He knew he shouldn't judge. But how could anyone with a soul take advantage of a woman as generous as her? And then it hit him as she rehashed the history with her late husband. Sadly, a wrongdoer like Jonathan knew exactly whom he was dealing with. He knew Katie's goodness could be exploited.

Anger kept rising in him, and he continued working to tamp it down. It especially wasn't easy when Katie's voice quaked.

"It's been hard for me to forgive Jonathan. But just as hard to forgive myself. My *mamm* and *daed* worked their whole lives to have a wonderful home for us. Their entire lives. And then, I made the mistake of marrying Jonathan. In less than two years, all they'd worked for was gone."

"Katie, you can't blame yourself for another person giving in to evil." He gazed at her.

"Nathan, I can see in your eyes that you feel for me."

"I feel for you because I care, Katie. You didn't deserve any of this to happen."

"But having you feel sorry for me isn't why I told you all of this."

He had no idea what she meant by that or how to respond.

"Remember that day when I thought someone was following me? And it turned out to be an acquaintance of yours?"

He chuckled slightly. "How could I forget?"

"I should've told you why I was nervous about that then. How I'd experienced strangers approaching me after Jonathan passed. But I didn't because I was protecting myself."

"I'm sorry, Katie, but I don't know what you mean."

"I was afraid for my job. I was scared that if you all knew how I'd been conned by Jonathan that you'd think I couldn't be trusted to run the market. That you'd be concerned and even fire me, thinking I could be easily deceived again."

"Oh, Katie. You're so perfect for the market and—" *me,* he almost added. "And we all have pasts. Hurtful as they can be, they're there to learn from."

"You sound like a wise old man, Nathan."

"You mean I can't be a smart young one?"

"Oh, I don't know. I suppose."

A smile lit her face, lifting his heart. So did the sound of her giggle.

"For sure and certain, it's been a day of surprises, hasn't it?" she asked.

"*Jah,* it has," he replied. And added to it was the letter from Shetler Homebuilders asking when he was returning. Also, unbelievably, a note from Helping Hands Christian Ministry inquiring if he was still available for rescue operations. It seemed both organizations knew his healing time was coming to an end. So was his time with Katie. Not that he wanted it to.

Looking her way, he couldn't help but gaze at her.

"Nathan…"

"Yes?" he replied, ready to do anything if she asked.

"Thank you," she said. "You've been so much to me. A shoulder to cry on. A person to turn to. Someone who cheers me on. And someone who knows what I love—"

What she loves? Did she mean who? He could only hope.

"Like art and animals," she continued. "And you're someone who surprises me by taking me to the best place ever. *Gott* gives me strength and you do too, Nathan. You make me believe I can make it on my own. And that's been my plan all along."

It wasn't that he wasn't happy for her. She really did deserve to feel good about herself and be able to move on. But it also wasn't what he wanted to hear.

All at once, his mind drifted to his own reality and the mail he'd received. Unfortunately, soon he'd have to respond.

Chapter Sixteen

Standing at the cash register, Katie glanced up at the clock on the market wall. She couldn't believe what she was seeing. But there it was. The minute hand was on twelve and the hour hand on five. It truly was the last hour of Nathan's last day. Their final time to be spent at the store together.

Thankfully, Barbara Glick and her sister Celeste had been working out just fine ever since they'd filled in a few days before. They'd caught on to everything quickly and both wanted to work part-time. That made it easy to create a schedule for the three of them.

Still…even with everything falling into place so nicely prior to Nathan's departure, a wave of melancholy washed over her. When she'd first met Nathan, she might've hoped he'd head out of town quickly. But now that he really was leaving, well, she couldn't imagine how it was going to feel without him. They'd spent so many hours at the market working, laughing, helping others and well, disagreeing some too. Yet with *Gott*'s help, they had restored the store together. That had been revitalizing for her too.

Sighing, she looked over at Nathan a couple of aisles away. Seeing the well-built man with his strong hands so carefully stocking the bread shelves, she couldn't escape the truth. It wasn't only at the market where she'd enjoyed being in his company.

Just watching him, her mind began to drift to so many times they'd shared…walks, talks, outings, game nights… and star-filled nights. Recalling the most recent of those moonlit evenings, she startled when a tap came on her shoulder. She turned to see one of the new workers.

"Katie, is it still all right if I leave early?" Barbara asked.

"Absolutely," Katie replied.

Barbara had offered to bring a broccoli salad to Nathan's surprise farewell get together at the inn and had confessed she'd not made it that morning before coming to the store. So she still had to pull it together. Mary Louise was ordering pizza from Bruno's, and Annie was baking Nathan's favorite red velvet cupcakes. Plus, her sister had made arrangements for a final softball game with him and the Glick kids. That was something they all knew he'd be sure to enjoy.

"And, Katie," Barbara continued. "Like Celeste and I said, we'll plan to open the store tomorrow morning. Just in case you want the time off to say more goodbyes."

Goodbye. Her heart clenched. In less than twenty-four hours, Nathan would be off on a rescue mission. And after that? There was no reason why Middlefield wouldn't be his next stop.

Something she didn't even want to think about now.

"*Danke*, Barbara. We'll see how it goes." She spoke casually, even though she totally planned on coming to work on time. Because work was good for the soul, wasn't it? Hadn't it gotten her this far? And it would positively be the best substitution when missing the only man that she'd ever gotten so close to.

* * *

Nathan wasn't surprised to see Barbara exit the market's door. But he was taken aback when his *Onkel* Jacob crossed the entrance at the same time. Hadn't they already said their goodbyes the evening before after dinner at Sylvia's house?

After giving Katie a quick hello, his white-bearded uncle shuffled directly toward him. Obviously, he had something on his mind. Nathan just couldn't conceive what.

"So, did you tell Katie?" his great uncle asked quietly. "And are you staying now?" His shaggy brows rose over his wire-rimmed glasses, appearing hopeful. "I have to know."

"*Onkel*, I have no idea what you're talking about."

His uncle waved a wrinkled hand. "Sure, you do. Last night when I said you and Katie make a *gut* team, I meant a *gut* couple too. I thought that might get you moving to tell her you love her."

Shocked, Nathan's head jerked. Immediately, he glanced at Katie, worried that she may be listening. Fortunately, she was busy tidying up the cash register area. Even so, he gently tugged on his uncle's arm, moving him closer.

"How do you know I feel that about her?"

Seeming annoyed, his uncle shook his head. "A man as old as I am can tell that about another man." He frowned. "So, you've never said how you feel?"

"Well, no, not exactly. I mean, I did tell her that she made me feel like Blossom Grove is home again."

"Hmph."

"But, *Onkel* Jacob, that's a big deal for me. I haven't felt like that in a lot of years."

"At least it's honest then." His uncle paused, then cringed. "You didn't go telling her things like being around her felt as good as sitting on the porch in a rocking chair, did you?"

"*Nee*, although that is a *gut* feeling. And she does make me feel that content sometimes."

"Really, Nathan?" *Onkel* Jacob's eyes grew wide. "You think that's what a woman wants to hear?"

Nathan peered over Jacob's shoulder at the sweet woman who'd captured his heart. He almost hesitated to say the next words out loud. "Do you mean I should just tell her that I love her?"

Onkel Jacob clapped his hands. "That's a start, and you may want to fill that in with a few other things."

"Like what?"

"Like what?" his uncle grumbled. "Like whatever else is on your heart." He tapped a finger into Nathan's chest. "Didn't being around me and your *aenti* Lovina all those years teach you anything?"

"I know you both laughed a lot." Nathan instantly smiled, remembering.

"Like I've seen you and Katie do."

"And you'd argue some too."

"In the friendliest most respectful way, like you and Katie do."

"True." Nathan nodded. "And then at the end of each work shift, I'd hear you and *Aenti* both thank *Gott* for the day...and each other." Nathan would never ever forget that.

Onkel Jacob clasped his shoulder. "And I hope you and Katie get to do the same. But you have to speak up, Nathan. Speak up and declare the feelings *Gott* has put inside you."

If only he could. But it wasn't that easy.

"*Onkel*, what you don't understand is that Katie doesn't seem interested in a relationship. Her past with men—well, it ain't so *gut*."

"Nathan." His uncle said his name solemnly. "All I know is this. Sometimes we humans regret things that we say.

But then, we find a way to make up for that. There's healing and we move on. But if there's something your heart is aching to say, and you don't get it out?" His uncle paused. "Well, I hate to tell you, but you could regret that for a *verra* long time."

With that, his uncle walked away and over to Katie. He overheard them both chuckling. Meanwhile, he couldn't move. Every joint in his body stiffened.

When his uncle had said "a *verra* long time"…could that mean the rest of his life?

Looking over at the woman he was so smitten with, he saw her pretty smile. He heard her sweet giggle. And again, he experienced the amazing way all those simplest of things about her made him feel. Without a doubt, he knew the answer to his own probing question.

He just didn't know if he'd have the nerve to share what was in his heart. And time was running out.

Chapter Seventeen

Nathan had truly appreciated the farewell dinner the ladies had put together. Annie's idea to host a friendly softball game for all of them had been kind of her too. Yet after
all was done, and he stood at the inn's open shed putting
away the baseball equipment, there was no doubt about it.
He might've been physically present for each event, but
ever since the earlier conversation with his great uncle, his
mind—and heart—had been elsewhere.

"Nathan, you forgot something."

At the sound of Katie's voice, he turned. How badly he
wanted to tell her that no, he hadn't forgotten. Not at all.
He hadn't forgotten her and never would. She was always
in his thoughts.

But how ridiculous would that sound when she was
merely holding up a baseball mitt he'd overlooked.

"Danke," he replied, taking the glove from her hand.
Swiveling around, he tossed it into its rightful container.
Then he stepped back and closed the shed door. But his
grasp lingered on the handle. His heart thumped crazily
in his chest.

It's now or never!

Now! he dared himself.

Circling back to her, he could feel his eyes grow wide as he sought hers.

"Katie, I didn't want to say this here. Not standing in front of Mary Louise's shed of all places. I pictured saying something to you with us sitting on a blanket high on a hill. Maybe we'd be overlooking Blossom Grove and then gazing at countless stars in the sky. Or we'd be back in the swing at Almond Creek. Or even just next to each other in the garden here." Words spouted out before he could stop himself. "But here we are. And this isn't easy to say, but the time has come. I can't wait any longer. I have to tell you—"

Initially, when he'd first started babbling, Katie's forehead creased. Then her expression softened, and a warm smile touched her lips. Had she guessed what he was about to say? And maybe she was even feeling the same way? It seemed a possibility when she took a step closer and touched his forearm.

"Nathan, it's *oll recht.* It's not always easy to tell someone goodbye. And there isn't a perfect place to say it, ain't so?"

"But, Katie, that's just it." He laid his hand over hers. "I don't want to say goodbye. Not to you. I don't want to leave you."

"Oh, Nathan…" She sighed. "You can't keep being concerned about me. In the short time we've been together, you've helped me and Annie so much. You've truly been a gift from *Gott*, and I'm much better now because of you. I know it's your nature, but I'm telling you—you don't have to rescue me any longer."

"Rescue *you*?" He shook his head. "Katie, you're an amazing woman. You're strong and bright. Hardworking. You're warmhearted and caring too. I agree, you don't need to be rescued. But the thing is, I do—or I did. And that's what you've done. I know I've said it before…but you've made this town feel like home to me again."

"But that's nothing to do with me," she countered. "That's your own doing…your own goodness. You resurrected your uncle's business. You've helped folks in the community. You made peace regarding your brother. And you even have Mrs. Hochstetler liking you again."

"Ha!" He chuckled wryly. "That only took saving her life."

"True." She giggled. "But it worked."

He hated to be serious while seeing the smile that rounded her cheeks. Even so, he boldly took her hand in his.

"The thing is… I don't think it would matter what town I'm in. If I were with you, Katie, it would feel like home to me. Because…because…"

Say it. Say it now.

"Because I love you."

There, he had said it. And then she slipped her hand right from his grasp. Her mouth dropped open. Her eyes flew wide. All leading him to rattle on some more.

"Believe me. I'm just as surprised as you are. This— these feelings for you, it's sure not what I'd planned."

Still, no reply. Only a stunned expression.

"I mean…" he yammered on. "I came back here wanting to leave Blossom Grove as fast as I could. But then my feelings for you…they just kept growing." He lifted his brows, hoping to hear the same from her.

Instead, she stood, blinking at him. "Oh, Nathan…" she murmured his name. "I—I don't know what to say."

Even though her blue eyes were set on his, his heart sank. That wasn't the reply he'd longed for.

"I only wish…" she started. And he heard a crack in her voice.

"Wish what?" he asked quietly.

"Nothing." She shook her head. "Nothing," she repeated. "Will you just hold me for a minute?" she whispered softly. "Just hug me in your arms?"

Wanting to give her anything she asked, he opened his arms to her. As she stepped into them, he caressed her and held her close. Gladness filled him when she seemed so at ease, her head snug against his chest. Until a somber recollection shot through him, and he remembered how days earlier they'd stood the same way on the inn's sidewalk. It also reminded him of all the horrific trials she'd been put through. All of which made him want to pull her closer. Hold her tighter. Feeling so much for her, he gently laid his head on top of hers. "It's okay, Katie. It's okay. You don't have to say a word."

The silence of the evening encircled them as they stood wrapped in each other's arms. Even if she couldn't declare her love for him, he would've still been happy to stay in that closeness for forever. But then, within minutes, she lifted her head and looked up at him.

"Nathan, after everything I put Annie through, I made a promise to myself before I came here. I vowed I wouldn't get involved in matters of the heart. Not ever again. And I can't back down on that. I just can't. For my sake and mostly for Annie's, I need to make it on my own." Tears glistened in her eyes as she spoke. "I care about you so much, and I hope you understand. I, uh, signed the rental agreement on the apartment. We're moving in next week. With *Gott*'s help, I'm going to keep working at making a life for us here—for Annie and me."

Although hurt and disappointment racked his chest, with the tip of his finger, he gently rubbed at a teardrop trickling down her cheek. As much as it was killing him to hear what she said, he spoke lovingly. "I respect that, Katie. I respect you. Maybe someday?"

"*Jah*, maybe someday." Her lips curved into the briefest smile before puckering up in sadness again.

"Katie, before you go, I just want to say it again. I love you, and if you don't love me, that's something I'll have to live with. But I'll be thinking of you and praying that you find the person of your heart. Someone who will love and cherish you because you deserve no less than that."

More tears flooded her cheeks as she stood on her tiptoes, gazing at him. He thought she was about to say something. But then, her lips lightly brushed against his cheek. A goodbye kiss, for sure. How could he expect anything more? He unwrapped his arms, letting loose of his hold on her. He had to let her go.

"*Gott* bless you, Nathan. I'll be praying for you too."

She started to walk away. He reached out and gently touched her arm.

"*Jah?*" she asked him.

"I just wanted one more chance to look at you. It may be forever till I see you again."

All at once, she stepped toward him. Ever so boldly yet ever so lightly, she drew his face toward hers. Then slowly, she lifted her lips to his. Her kiss was as warm and sweet as he'd ever imagined it would be. He only wished it could last longer...even forever.

"I'll never forget you, Nathan," she said as she backed away from him. "Never."

At least there was that, he thought, as she turned from him and he watched her walk away. Because as *Gott* was his witness, there was no question about it. He'd never forget her either.

Chapter Eighteen

Lying in bed, Katie was thankful the morning sun was shining so brightly through the window. If it hadn't been, she would've felt entirely lifeless. As it was, saying good-bye to Nathan the night before had taken a toll on her. Even more than she'd expected. Knowing Barbara and Celeste would open the market in her absence, she'd lingered longer in bed than usual.

At least long enough until she heard Nathan slip out the inn's front door, headed for the bus stop.

But one glance at her alarm clock told her she couldn't put off experiencing life without him another minute. Even Annie had gotten up before her.

Determinedly, she rose and began her getting-ready-for-work routine. She plodded down the hall to the bathroom, washed her face, brushed her teeth. Then trailed back to the bedroom where she slipped on a clean dress. She combed and coiled her blond hair. Donned her *kapp*. Tied on an apron. Put on her shoes. And lastly, about to slide her notebook into her apron pocket as she did each day. But—where was it? She frowned, scanning its usual place on top of the dresser.

Bending down, she peeked under the dresser, trying to find it. Standing back up, she searched through the drawers.

When she still came up empty, she was completely flummoxed. Had she been so distressed the evening before that she'd left it somewhere downstairs?

Yet after heading down to the entryway, there was still no sign of her notebook. Perplexed, she made her way into the dining room. There sat Annie at the table with half a glass of orange juice and an empty cereal bowl in front of her. Her sister had sure gotten an unusually early start, hadn't she? That was puzzling itself.

"*Guder mariye*, Annie. Have you seen—"

"Your notebook?" Annie held up the pocket-sized booklet with a smug smile.

"*Jah*, that. I need it before I head to work." She stretched out her hand to grasp the book. Annie pulled it away beyond her reach.

"Oh, you need it all right," her sister replied. "But for now, why don't you have a seat?"

"Annie..." Katie took a deep breath, trying to keep her patience. "I don't understand what you're up to, but I have to get going."

"You'll understand in a minute. After you take this little test that I have for you."

"A test? Annie, really, I'm not in the mood."

"Katie." Her sister barked her name. "You tell me what's best for me all the time. Now I'm trying to do what's best for you." She huffed. "This won't take long. In fact, it can't take long. Please, sit."

Still clueless about whatever Annie was up to, she gave in and sat.

"Now..." Annie started. "Since you're the one who's always saying you're going by the book—and not your heart—well, I have a few questions for you in this little notebook of yours."

"Questions?" Katie narrowed her eyes. "Annie, please—"

"Shush!" Annie demanded, pointing a finger at her. Then she cleared her throat. "All right. My first question. Do you find Nathan Bowman to be easy on the eyes?"

"This test is about Nathan?" Katie winced.

"Just answer the question."

"Well, of course he is in his own rugged way. I mean, it wouldn't hurt if he'd shave more often. And he could try a different color of shirt besides white sometimes. But *jah*. His blue eyes sort of hug you and the lines around them are interesting. And then his jawline is perfect and strong-looking. And his smile…well, it makes you smile, doesn't it?"

"Okay. Good answer. That's a definite yes." Right away, Annie removed the pencil tucked behind her ear. She made a check mark in the notebook. Then she continued. "Question number two. Is Nathan the kindest man that you've ever met?"

"Annie, why are you asking about—"

Again, Annie interrupted her. "Just answer the question, please."

"Do you mean the kindest man besides our *daed*?"

Annie nodded.

"Then I have to say yes."

"Gut, gut." Her sister beamed, penciling in another check mark. "Now for the next question. Do you believe Nathan is the kind of man a woman can trust her heart to?"

All at once, Katie felt her pulse quicken. "Trusting isn't easy."

"But everyone has to do it in this life or not have a life." Her sister had turned sage-like on her once again. "So, what's your answer—yes or no?"

Katie bit her lip, hesitating. Then let out a deep breath. "I don't have any reason to say *nee* to that about him."

"Yay!" Annie yipped. "So that's a yes." She swiftly jotted on the page. "Okay, a few more questions to go. Next one is, if you were ever hurting in any way, do you believe Nathan would be there for you?"

Instantaneously, the question triggered a rush of sweet memories. Recalling every way that he'd already been there for her, she felt a lump rise in her throat. She swallowed hard before answering. "Of course. Yes, he would."

"That's a big check mark." Annie penciled it in. "And, the follow-up is, has Nathan said how much he cares about you?"

"Why do I have a feeling you already know the answer to this?"

Annie shrugged innocently.

"Annie…" Katie drew out her name.

"I may have overheard something."

"May have?" Katie quirked a brow.

"No harm done. It just means we both know that's also a yes." She scribbled on the paper. "Now, we're almost finished. Next, do you find Nathan to be an affectionate man?"

Right away, Katie's cheeks heated. The answer obviously revealed itself.

Annie giggled as her eyes lit up. "Really, *schweschder*? Have you hugged him? Kissed him?"

"That wasn't the original question."

"Ha. You're right. But I'm guessing that's a yes too." Annie made two check marks. "And the final question." Annie's voice softened. "Do you, Katie, wish you had more time to spend with Nathan? More hours, days, months, years?"

Before Katie could begin to rein in her emotions, tears dotted her eyes. And began to slide down her cheeks.

Annie placed a caring hand over hers. "Then you can't

let him go, Katie. At least not without telling him. We need to leave now. We need to get you to him."

Katie swiped at her cheeks. "Annie, I can't."

"*Jah*, you can." Annie held up the booklet. "Because it's all right here. Everything in this notebook of yours—that you trust so much—says your heart should be with his."

"But I messed up so badly before. How can you forget what I got us into? I can't do that again. I need to protect you."

"Protect me? From what? A wonderful person like Nathan?"

"Maybe he's too good to be true, Annie. I could be fooled again."

"Well, I can't. So, you don't have to worry about protecting me. Or is it you? Are you afraid you might get hurt again?"

"I don't know, Annie." Katie sniffled, truly confused. "I need air." She rose from the chair. "I need to think."

"Well, don't think too long." Annie glanced at the clock. "Or it could be too late."

Her sister's warning echoed in her mind as she shambled out to the garden. Embarrassed by her wet cheeks, she wiped them quickly as soon as she saw Mary Louise. With a watering can in her hands, giving the flowers an early morning drink, her friend warmly greeted her like always.

"Mary Louise, did you know what Annie was up to?"

"I did." Mary Louise paused from her task, gripping the can with two hands in front of her.

"What do you think?"

"It's not what *I* think, sweet *maedel*."

Feeling bewildered, Katie glanced down. As she did, a colorful metal sign poking out of the ground stared back at her. She'd seen it plenty but had never taken the time to really look at it before. "'What you water grows.'" She read the sentence surrounded by painted flowers. "I'm thinking that's not just about plants, is it?"

"No it isn't." Mary Louise offered a comforting smile. "But it took me a while to come to terms with that too." She sighed. "Thomas bought me the same kind of sign when we first took over the inn. Over time, it got weathered and rusty. The paint chipped away. Years ago, after his passing, a friend of mine noticed and got me this new sign. But for the longest time, I couldn't get rid of the one Thomas had gotten for me. I was watering the pain of losing him so to speak. Until I realized, he and *Gott* would want me to be renewed and would want me to move on."

"Hmm…" Katie uttered quietly, though her heart was frantically racing. "It's just… I'm scared, Mary Louise."

"Love can do that to a person, for sure." A motherly understanding shone in Mary Louise's eyes. "Yet with the right person, it can make you blossom in ways you never knew possible. But again, Katie, it's your choice. Water fear? Or water the possibility of happiness?"

"He could already be gone."

"The bus doesn't stop for him for another half hour."

"Then…" She straightened her shoulders. And swallowed hard. "Then I need to go to him."

A look of joy instantly gleamed in Mary Louise's eyes. She tossed the watering can aside. "Oh, how I was praying you'd say that! Rusty is already out front and ready to go."

Apparently, Annie must've been listening through the screened window. She ran out the door, squealing. As her sister looped one arm through hers, Mary Louise took hold of her other.

"You girls are serious." Katie laughed.

"When it comes to your heart—" Mary Louise said.

"And your happily-ever-after—" Annie chimed in.

"*Jah*, we are," the two of them exclaimed in unison.

Nathan knew his great uncle had been right. He would've regretted not telling Katie that he loved her. Even so, as he sat on the bench at the bus stop, it still stung that he hadn't heard the same from her. He could only hope once he was gone from Blossom Grove, the aching inside him would ease some.

Looking down the road, he longed to see the vehicle that would transport him and his heart. It couldn't come quickly enough. But just as he did, a familiar-looking creature came into view. Or was he just imagining it? Jumping to his feet, he took another look.

Rusty!

At once, his heart leaped. Then he became anxious as the buggy halted in front of him. All three gals that he'd come to know so well and care for hopped out.

"What's wrong?" he asked. "Do you all need some help?"

At first, Katie came running up to him. Until she stopped a foot away, suddenly appearing unusually shy.

"Seriously, Katie, is everything *oll recht*?"

"I hope you'll think so, Nathan." She began wringing her hands. "Because I want to say that being with you—well, it makes me feel like I'm home too."

"Really?" Was he hearing right?

"*Jah*, Nathan, I love you. I've known it for a while. I was just afraid to say the words out loud."

All the heaviness he'd been feeling lifted as he pulled her into his arms. "Katie, I don't have to go. I don't have to leave you."

"*Jah*, you do." She gazed into his eyes. "You have to go

rescue someone's loved one, just like you rescued me. Just make me one promise." Her voice was soft, undemanding.

"What's that?"

"That you'll come back."

"Always, Katie, always—if you promise to be here for me."

"Oh, I will."

Out of the corner of his eye, he saw the bus headed their way. Even so, there was still time. Pulling off his hat, he held it at the side of their faces. It wasn't much privacy, but enough. He sought her lips and kissed her, feeling blessed and thankful. It might've only been one kiss. But it was the promise of so many more to come. So very many more.

As Mary Louise headed Rusty back to the inn, Katie touched her lips for the dozenth time and couldn't stop smiling.

She'd noticed her innkeeper friend had been grinning plenty too, and an excited Annie leaned forward from the back seat.

"I know what I want to be when I grow up," Annie said happily.

Katie glanced at Mary Louise and could tell she didn't know what to expect from her sister either.

"What's that, Annie?" Katie asked.

"I'm going to be a matchmaker like Mary Louise."

Katie watched Mary Louise peek over her shoulder, giving her sister a warm smile. "Oh, I just have a way of bringing people together. The inn is *gut* for that."

Katie's ears perked up at that. "You mean you purposely had me and Nathan stay there at the same time?"

Mary Louise shrugged. "I had a feeling you two might be a good fit for each other. But also, let me tell you both, and, Annie, especially you, if you're going to be a match-maker—I always ask for *Gott*'s guidance because—"

"He's the best matchmaker of all," Katie and Annie chimed together.

They all chuckled as Mary Louise pulled up to the inn. Slipping out of the buggy, Katie glimpsed the baby blue and white Happy Endings sign. The first day she and Annie arrived at the inn, she'd inwardly scoffed at the signage. It wasn't just the name, which seemed as wistful as a fairy tale, that had struck her numb self then. It was also the bow painted beneath the name that seemed to foolishly say all the loose ends and hurts in life could be tied up and made pretty that way. But for a while now, she'd been seeing the sign so differently. In her mind, it read Hopeful New Beginnings.

After thanking and hugging Annie and Mary Louise, it was time to get to work. Her steps felt light as ever as she strode down the sidewalk toward Miller's Market. She might've been alone, but the love in her heart she felt for Nathan—well, it made her feel like he was right by her side.

Epilogue

Five months later...and two days before the Troyer-Bowman Wedding

Katie had never seen the Happy Endings Inn decked out in autumn. But she should have known Mary Louise would have the place looking just as beautiful and inviting as during the spring and summer. Vases and baskets filled with every color of chrysanthemum—red, orange, yellow, pink, purple and white—decorated each room. All placed there to create a lovely atmosphere for a pre-wedding dinner with Nathan's family. That group included his parents, his sister's and brother's families, his *Onkel* Jacob, Sylvia and Clyde—and Mary Louise, of course—who were all just as colorful as the flora. Delightful chatter and laughter continued nonstop, coming from all directions.

"Schweschder." Annie scurried over to her, wearing the huge grin Katie always loved to see. "Did you hear what Nathan's sister, Betsy, said?"

"Nee, I didn't. But from that smile of yours, it must've been something good."

"She introduced me to her *kinner* as their cousin Annie." Her sister practically swooned. "And then Celia did the same with her little ones. That means I have cousins now,

Katie. Can you believe it?" Annie's voice squeaked. "I guess it means I have *aentis* and *onkels* too." She beamed.

"It's *wunderbaar*, isn't it?" Katie hugged her. "Not only do we have each other, but we have so much family now, including Mary Louise."

"For sure and certain, *Mamm* and *Daed* would've liked each and every one of them."

"*Jah*, I'd been thinking that too. They truly would have."

"And, they'd be happy that we have a new home now."

The generosity of Nathan's relatives had been overwhelming. For a wedding gift, his *Onkel* Jacob was giving them ownership of the market with a percentage of the profits going to him. And with Barbara and Celeste still working part-time, she and Nathan would have a little time to themselves occasionally. Maybe even time to start a family.

Plus, they didn't need to worry about where they'd be living. Since his parents wanted to travel, they were eager to move into the *dawdi haus* on their property, letting the newlyweds maintain the house Nathan grew up in.

"And you'll have your own bedroom again for a change," Katie replied.

"Thankfully." Annie sighed. "By the way, does Nathan know you snore?"

Katie jerked. "I do not snore."

"If you say so." Annie chuckled. "Also, their house isn't too far from Marcus Yoder's home."

"Marcus who?" Katie blinked. Though she didn't know why she was surprised. Annie had moved on from Andrew months before, meeting more boys and girls her own age at worship.

"Just a boy I know." Annie waved her hand, appearing eager to change the subject. "Oh, and Nathan's mom is going to help Mary Louise and me with the celery table decorations for your wedding."

Just hearing the joy in her sister's voice, Katie could feel a well of emotion rising in her throat.

Gott, you're too good to me.

"I'm going to go see if my aunts need any help with my young cousins." Annie giggled before heading to the other side of the room.

Watching her sister nearly skip over to her "cousins," Katie knew what she needed to do. Seeing all the happiness surrounding them and feeling overcome with joy herself, she wanted nothing more than to go to the prayer box at the entrance of the inn. Surprisingly, she found Nathan already there at work.

"Are you penning a prayer, asking *Gott* to get you out of this before it's too late?" she teased.

He laughed. "No, but are you about to do that?"

"Never. I just wanted to write a prayer of thanks."

"Me too. In fact, I was writing one from both of us. Let me know what you think," he said, handing her a slip of paper to read.

Dear Gott,

During all the years that I enjoyed being at Happy Endings, and all the times that Katie's mamm *talked about Blossom Grove, You knew we'd be here together one day, rescuing each other's hearts. What can we say but* danke? *Thank you for loving us the way You do. Thank you for the joy of loving each other. May we bring You smiles and glory all our lives together.*

Yours always, Nathan and Katie.

"It's perfect." She blinked back the moisture in her eyes as she folded the paper. Then placed it in the wooden box.

"Perfect, like you are for me." Coming close, Nathan lifted her chin. She could tell he was intent on placing a sweet kiss on her lips. Until a clap startled them both. And there stood Annie with her hands on her hips.

"You two will have plenty of time for kissing later. All your lives, in fact. Right now, you need to get going," she announced. "The family is ready to eat."

* * * * *

Dear Reader,

I hope you enjoyed your visit to Blossom Grove! After I'd written Katie and Nathan's story, a long-ago friend of mine came to mind. She'd always had the details of how she'd find her lifelong partner perfectly arranged in her head. She had a list of dealbreakers, and just like Katie, she vowed never to trust a man with her heart again.

As in, she was *never* going to date a man she worked with, *never* going to date a divorced man, and *never* going to date a man with children.

So, when a man began working in her department and asked her out, she emphatically said no!

Until she was laid off from her job. And he called to see how she was doing. Then he called again and asked her to meet him for lunch. Soon it was lunches, dinners and breakfasts after church. And even though they weren't co-workers any longer, she'd learned other things about him like he was divorced and a father of one. Always and forever, she said she'd never date that type of man.

So, they stopped dating. And instead, they got married!

Time and again, I have to remind myself of how silly I am to put limitations on God's never-ending supply of unlimited possibilities. After all, wouldn't the Creator of the entire universe, who also formed our hearts with His own hands, know best what will fill our hearts with happiness? When it came to Katie and Nathan, that was surely the case.

I hope you enjoyed their story. And if you'd like to say hello sometime, I'd love to hear from you. My website is www.cathyliggett.com or please visit me on Facebook.

Blessings now and always,
Cathy

Harlequin® Reader Service

Enjoyed your book?

Try the perfect subscription for Romance readers and get more great books like this delivered right to your door.

See why over 10+ million readers have tried Harlequin Reader Service.

Start with a Free Welcome Collection with free books and a gift—valued over $20.

Choose any series in print or ebook. See website for details and order today:

TryReaderService.com/subscriptions